D1093675

Moon WITHOUT Magic

OTHER BOOKS BY MICHAEL O. TUNNELL

WISHING MOON

THE PRYDAIN COMPANION

SCHOOL SPIRITS

BROTHERS IN VALOR:
A STORY OF RESISTANCE

THE CHILDREN OF TOPAZ

MICHAEL O. TUNNELL

DUTTON CHILDREN'S BOOKS

DUTTON CHILDREN'S BOOKS
A division of Penguin Young Readers Group

Published by the Penguin Group
Penguin Group (USA) Inc., 375 Hudson Street, New York, New York 10014, U.S.A.
Penguin Group (Canada), 90 Eglinton Avenue East, Suite 700, Toronto, Ontario, Canada
M4P 2Y3 (a division of Pearson Penguin Canada Inc.) • Penguin Books Ltd, 80 Strand,
London WC2R 0RL, England • Penguin Ireland, 25 St Stephen's Green, Dublin 2, Ireland
(a division of Penguin Books Ltd) • Penguin Group (Australia), 250 Camberwell Road, Camberwell,
Victoria 3124, Australia (a division of Pearson Australia Group Pty Ltd)
Penguin Books India Pvt Ltd, 11 Community Centre, Panchsheel Park,
New Delhi - 110 017, India • Penguin Group (NZ), 67 Apollo Drive, Rosedale, North
Shore 0745, Auckland, New Zealand (a division of Pearson New Zealand Ltd)
Penguin Books (South Africa) (Pty) Ltd, 24 Sturdee Avenue, Rosebank,
Johannesburg 2196, South Africa

Penguin Books Ltd, Registered Offices: 80 Strand, London WC2R 0RL, England

CIP Data is available.

Published in the United States by Dutton Children's Books,
a division of Penguin Young Readers Group
345 Hudson Street, New York, New York 10014
www.penguin.com/youngreaders

Designed by Tim Hall and Beth Herzog   •   Printed in USA
ISBN: 978-0-525-47729-7
First Edition
1 3 5 7 9 10 8 6 4 2

FOR SYDNEY, RILEY, KELSEY,
AND JACE

Moon WITHOUT Magic

Prologue

What know you of magic lamps—of the demon jinn who dwell within brass walls? Draw near, my friends, and I, Idris—the master spinner of tales—will amaze you with a saga the likes of which you've never heard.

What is that you say? This is merely a child's bedtime story? No, my friends, I have seen such a lamp! Have worked its dark enchantments!

You laugh, but this is no jest. My tale is truth. Dangerous truth for my newfound family—a family forged by this marvelous, yet dreadful lamp. Even you, my intrepid listeners, may find this knowledge too perilous to possess. Will my tale excite you? Please you? Yes, indeed! But if you are faint of heart, now is the time to leave me. Good! I see you are to a soul a brave lot.

I call my tale "The Maiden and the Moon Without Magic"—and it is as much the story of my own failings as it is a story of love, magic, and intrigue.

I was once a poor orphan living alone in one of the great eastern cities. It was there I met a girl as beautiful as all the stars in the heavens. I will simply call her "A" for her protection. She was an orphan, too, and worse, a beggar living in the streets. But she was as generous and kind a girl as will ever live.

How did I meet her? Why, I saved her life! I leapt between this flower of all flowers and the Sultan's henchmen, and with the cunning words of a storyteller, I distracted them from their prey. I befuddled the Sultan's guards, spiriting A away. And that day she took me in.

You may ask, "How is it possible that a homeless beggar girl would take in a stray cat, much less an orphan boy?" Magic made this possible, my friends! An enchanted lamp—newly come into her possession—changed her fortune and mine. But months passed before I came to understand the power that had fallen into A's hands—or should I say onto her head?

Oh, I did not misspeak! The lamp came first to the girl's forehead, and it knocked her to the ground, senseless. The Sultan's daughter—the Princess—had hurled it in anger to drive away the waif. And though her aim was true, she had unknowingly tossed away a matchless treasure.

The lamp was but a dented bit of brass and seemed of little value, but it belonged to the Princess's new husband. Who knows where or how he came by his magical trinket, though oddly enough he did not seem to miss it. But not so the Princess! Once she discovered her folly, I believe she might gladly have slaughtered every beggar girl in the city to retrieve the lost prize. Little did I know the

Sultan's guards were searching for the lamp when I rescued A from their clutches.

And so I lived with my flower of all flowers in a spacious estate jinni gold had purchased. Other friends found their way to us, and we became a family of sorts. And though we had most everything one could dream of, I cannot say we lived happily. At least, I did not, because A and I lived separate lives. And when I realized she could not love me as I loved her, I adopted the life I now lead, that of an itinerant storyteller.

However, I did not stop caring for A. When the Princess and the palace guards discovered her whereabouts, I was there to save her once again—but this time I employed the enchanted lamp rather than a smooth tongue! A's gentle heart could not conceive of using the jinni's power against the Princess, but now I had learned the lamp's secret. At the last second—at the very moment the bloodletting had begun—I found a way to turn the demon's enchantments against the Princess. With a wish, I whisked the Sultan's daughter and her men a thousand leagues away to this very city, the city of Makkah.

There was true evil in the Princess. Therefore, removing her to the holiest of cities seemed a grand joke. But I was soon to see that I had been more stupid than clever. By sad chance, I had placed A in great peril yet again.

Once the Princess was gone, my lovely flower and our "family" moved away to a distant place. Caring for A too much to stay with her, I took to the desert tracks that led from city to city. My intention was to travel to Makkah. I did not consider the possibility of encountering the Princess, though I had sent her there. No, the decision to visit Makkah was Allah's inspiration—a white-hot desire for pilgrimage to the holy city.

After attending to the sacred sites, I planned to stay and hone my craft, telling stories to other faithful travelers. But alas, I did not make the pilgrimage. Instead, the Princess and her dark designs fell into my lap. Oh, what terrible choices then lay before me!

But for the intervening hand of the great Allah, I would not have known the Princess was returning home with a frightening new weapon—a terrifying power at her fingertips. And so, before even setting foot in the holy city, I found myself drawn homeward in the Princess's wake. Yet again I had been called on to deliver A from destruction. In a desperate moment of decision, I chose the first opportunity to save her that presented itself. Until then I had failed to devise a plan of any sort—other than the insane thought of murdering the Princess.

And now, this is where my tale truly begins. Though I have never killed another human, in hindsight it might have been the better choice. When the story is ended, you must be the judge.

ONE

"AMINAH, MY DEAR, that demon robe is up to something new every time you wrap yourself in it," said Hassan. "Remember that first night you appeared in my bakery? I nearly leapt out of my skin at the sight of you, and in those days the robe did little more than glow with an eerie light." He moved close and, with a tentative finger, stroked her cheek. "Now—well, it's quite frightening."

"Frightening? Just because it snapped at you once?" Aminah smiled and shook her head, reaching up to take his hand in hers. "It was only having a little fun," she said.

"Hmmph," Hassan muttered. "It's unnerving when a robe suddenly growls, then lunges at you with the fangs of a lion. I swear it nipped me."

Aminah laughed. "My thawb does not bite. You just don't like magic."

"No, your thawb just doesn't like me. I think it's jealous. Doesn't that worry you? A jealous robe?" Hassan grimaced. "Imagine if someone were outside the window listening. In no time, I'd be branded Tyre's town idiot, and my bakery would be out of business."

Aminah giggled, then turned to gaze out a tall, peaked window. Though her new home mirrored the old estate in Al-Kal'as, this one was perched on a hillock south of Tyre that overlooked the sea.

"I never tire of watching these sunsets," she said. "Coming here was the right thing to do, don't you think?"

"Yes, of course," Hassan answered, encircling her with his arms and peering over her shoulder at the shimmering seascape. They stood quietly while the sun, like a great flaming pomegranate, quenched itself in the waves.

Aminah broke their comfortable silence. "Barra must wonder where we are. Our supper's waiting on the terrace."

As they turned to go, Hassan spoke, his voice almost a whisper. "It changes how you look, Aminah."

She sighed. "I thought we'd finished with the thawb."

"I watched you in the scrying orb when you visited that girl—Ella," he said. "You were fat. And . . . old."

"Perhaps you shouldn't peer into the orb, if it upsets you." Aminah sighed again. "Yes, it sometimes changes my appearance. The thawb has power to make me look exactly like Ella—or anyone else—thinks I should look. Ella thinks I'm her fairy godmother—whatever that's supposed to be. I suppose she has her own ideas how these fairy godmothers look, and the thawb is accommodating her. It's really very useful, when you think about it."

"I know you're doing marvelous work with the lamp and Jinni's magic, but don't you think we could be happy without enchantments? Magic has a way of causing trouble. Princess Badr tried to kill you for that lamp."

"But what about Ahab and his orphans?" Aminah cried, stamping her foot. "Because my wish enchanted a poor tailor's fingers, he's rich as a sultan and able to care for hundreds of abandoned children. It's just three wishes each full moon, Hassan. It only takes a little time to do good things."

Hassan raised his hands, as if to fend her off, and Aminah laughed. "I didn't mean you should get rid of the lamp," he said. "I'm only suggesting that you put it away. As long as the lamp is still yours, Ahab's gifts remain."

She stretched up on her toes and kissed him. "Badr will never find us, so stop worrying. The lamp saved me from starving, remember? In return I promised Allah that I would use it to make a difference in the world. And don't forget that *you* benefited from my promise, too."

Now it was Hassan's turn to sigh. "I hope you know what you're doing with Ella. Instead of wishing for those enchanted glass slippers, why not be more direct? Wish the girl a love spell to catch her prince."

"Love spells don't last. I learned that with Ahab and Khalidah. If I'd wished for a spell to bring them together, Ahab's orphans would still be without a new mother. Love is its own magic, Hassan. Haven't we discovered that for ourselves?"

"Yes," he answered softly.

"The night of the first ball, I could sense—rather, the orb

could sense—that Prince Louis would love Ella, given a little time. The slipper will simply bring them together."

"Well, even if you are addicted to magic," said Hassan, "I have to admit you know your business."

Aminah gaped at him in surprise. "You think I'm addicted to magic?" She laughed. "That's ridiculous."

"Then give it up. Jinni wouldn't mind. He'd be content to lounge about outside the lamp—eating, drinking, playing chess."

"No! Haven't you been listening? I have a commitment to keep."

He folded her in his arms again, kissing the furrow worrying her brow. "Forget what I said. I'm foolishly in love and jealous of anything that competes for your attention—whether it be magic or . . . or Ahab and Ella. Forgive me."

Aminah nestled against his chest for a moment, and then pushed away, tugging on his arm. "Come, or Jinni will have eaten everything."

When they reached the rooftop terrace, Barra had already lit the lamps and laid out her usual feast. The older woman's graying hair stirred in the sea breeze as she stared out across the dimly lit water. She turned at their step and smiled. "I was about to come for you."

Her smile was a mother's smile, the sight of which brought a happy lump to Aminah's throat. The day kind and selfless Barra had appeared at her gate in Al-Kal'as was the day she'd stopped being an orphan.

"Where's Jinni?" asked Hassan.

"Oh, no!" cried Aminah. "It's his day to stay in the lamp. I forgot to call him out."

"Poor Jinni," said Barra, looking mournful. "Is this weekly torture really necessary, Aminah?"

"You're too softhearted, Barra," said Hassan. "Though he makes himself look like our good old Uncle Omar, he's still a bottle imp. Sometimes I think he ought to have another day or two inside."

Barra bristled until she saw Hassan's grin. "Oh, you." She laughed. "You still haven't forgiven Jinni for not approving of you at first."

"He wouldn't have approved of anyone. He was jealous," said Hassan.

"Barra, do you really think I'm torturing Jinni?" asked Aminah, her eyes wide. "A day each week inside the lamp was his idea, you know. Neither he nor I can ever again forget he's a demon."

"No, no," Barra said, coming forward to hold Aminah's face in her hands. "Hassan's right. I've a soft spot for the old bottle imp. Now go on, let him out before everything cools."

Aminah hurried back to her apartment and approached a sandalwood wall panel. She slid it noiselessly aside, revealing an iron door. The door and the closet behind it were perfect duplicates of the ones in her old house—the secret place where she kept her treasures. Rotating small disks on the iron surface, she aligned the right combination of symbols and the door opened.

Inside, the shelves contained not only the lamp but also the scrying orb—the magical glass ball that had located and chosen Ahab, Hassan, and Ella to be blessed by Aminah's wishes. They also held her small, enchanted money chest that routinely replenished its own supply of gold coins, as well as a jewel-studded waterskin Hassan had gifted her when they first met in Al-Kal'as. The enchanted thawb sewn for her by Ahab the tailor—the one that so worried Hassan—hung from a hook.

Aminah carried the brass lamp out into her apartment and then rubbed its battered surface with a few brisk strokes. A dark substance—sludgelike and the color of a deep bruise—oozed from the lamp's spout. When the flow stopped, a sizable puddle had formed on the tiles, and it lay there, unmoving. Just when Aminah was about to poke at the sludge with her finger, it exploded in her face, and with a screech, she toppled back, sitting down hard on the floor. The explosion created a billowing purple cloud that filled the room, but in an instant it cleared, leaving a scowling Jinni behind. Bare-chested and turbaned, he stood with arms crossed and legs apart.

"That was a nasty trick," Aminah complained. "I thought you were beyond such behavior."

"Simply a bit of demon fun," said Jinni. "You are anxious for me to remember who I really am, and this proves I have not forgotten. Why are you grumbling? You *are* unscathed, after all."

"Tell that to my bottom. I landed hard enough to break something."

"My apologies." Jinni bowed. "Too much time inside the lamp, I suppose. I come out feeling mischievous."

"One day a week is too much time?" she asked. "Barra thinks I'm torturing you. I'm not, am I?"

"Perhaps a bit," he answered, his face solemn. Then, at Aminah's horrified expression, his deep, hollow laugh shook the room. "No, no, Mistress. It is as it should be. And I do not mind spending each night inside the lamp, either."

"Please tell Barra that," she said. "I don't want her thinking I'm a demon, too. By the way, I've come to fetch you for supper."

Jinni's eyes glowed. "Lead the way, oh merciful Master. Barra's magic awaits us!"

As they left the apartment, Aminah said, "Your new week outside the lamp is beginning, so I need to have your promise once again. Will you stay within the walls of the estate?"

Jinni wore a pained expression. "You ask me that every week. And I always answer that I will not pass through the portals, except in your company. Then you say, 'Nor shall you fly over the walls or dig beneath them or whisk yourself away with magic.' And then I say, 'Must I retain the shape and hue of a jinni?' And then you say, 'Yes, except when you are alone with Barra. Then you may assume the visage of Uncle Omar.' And then I say—"

"Stop! Do I really sound like that?" asked Aminah. Jinni had imitated her voice perfectly, though adding a whining tone she didn't think was hers. When he didn't answer, she laughed. "Fine, I trust you."

The demon bowed. "I am ever the slave between thy hands," he said with a grin.

"Good, for we visit Ella again tonight, and I need you to be particularly cooperative."

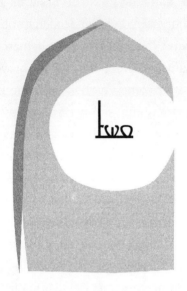

two

PRINCESS BADR AL-BUDUR flung the brass lamp across the room. Oil sprayed in its wake, and it struck the wall with a dull thud before clattering across the floor. The very sight of brass lamps infuriated her.

This was but one of many unhappy nights she had now spent in Makkah—an unscheduled visit that had been beyond her control. And because the Princess hated not being in control, she retrieved the dented lamp and threw it again. She cared not that her temper tantrum might awaken the entire khan, and, indeed, the innkeeper was soon calling softly at her door. She crossed his palm with a golden dinar, dismissing him with no other explanation, and settled among the silken cushions of her bed to sulk.

How had this happened? How had she ended up a thousand leagues from home? "Aminah," she said aloud, wincing at the sound of the name. She had had the beggar girl cornered—the one who had taken her feebleminded husband's enchanted lamp (never mind that she herself had thrown it at the urchin). The girl and the lamp had all but been in her clutches. Then, between one breath and another, Badr found herself and her guards wandering the streets of Makkah. Though the Princess was certain it been Aminah's doing, how the beggar girl had managed such a feat without calling upon the lamp's jinni remained a mystery.

Badr's rage had only been fed by the embarrassment of appearing in the holy city with nothing more than the robes in which she was draped. Had she not been a sultan's daughter, her situation would have been hopeless. Still, having to seek help from Makkah's governor had been humiliating. To save face, she'd fabricated the story of a horde of bandits who had robbed her of everything.

Badr al-Budur brooded through the night, anxious for the amber glow of morning. There was still a way to crush Aminah and reclaim the lamp, and by happenstance, she had stumbled upon it. If the stories were true, the secret was waiting for her but a day's journey to the west.

At dawn, the Princess roused her men and pushed them toward the port city of Juddah. By nightfall, they'd stabled their mounts at the town's finest khan and settled into their rooms. Badr allowed the men half an hour for supper, and then, following the innkeeper's directions, she guided her small band to the outskirts of the city.

Derelict buildings hugged narrow alleyways that were eerily

deserted, and the Princess wondered if the innkeeper might be mistaken. It seemed an odd sort of place to find such a great source of power. *Wealth accompanies power, does it not?* Badr thought. Yet they searched in a place of filth and poverty.

Their lamp flickered, almost guttering, and Saladin, the Captain of the Guard, cupped the flame in his hand, steadying it. The night was moonless, the streets of Juddah a black maze, and they could ill afford to lose their only light. He checked the oil—there was enough—then held a scrap of parchment near the flame. "According to the innkeeper's map, we take the next turn, to the right," Saladin whispered to the Princess.

The next turn deposited them in an alley no wider than Badr's arm span. It ended at a set of crumbling steps that led to an iron door.

"Wait here," Saladin ordered his men.

Badr had already mounted the steps and stood pounding at the door. The pitted, rust-eaten surface scraped the side of her tiny fist, staining it red. "Ashraf, the Wise," she called. "Open for Princess Badr al-Budur, the Full Moon of Full Moons, the daughter of the Sultan of Al-Kal'as."

The soft breezes that had earlier threatened their light suddenly joined forces, snuffing out the lamp. As Badr groped her way back to Saladin, she heard the door's arthritic metal hinges protesting in the darkness. An equally rickety voice, creaking with age, whispered from atop the steps.

"Only the Princess may enter."

"She will not enter without me," said Saladin.

"Then our interview has ended."

"No!" Badr called out. "I will come alone."

She silenced Saladin with a light touch to his cheek and

mounted the stairs. Again, the shrieking of corroded iron assaulted their ears, and the door was soon bolted against Saladin and his men.

Once inside, Badr heard the striking of flint and in a moment a wizened face peered at her over a lighted lamp. "I am not accustomed to being ordered about like a common street vendor," said Badr, in an icy effort to quash the tremor that threatened her voice.

"Follow," the man said, and without another glance, made his way up a flight of stairs and disappeared through another door. Badr had little choice but to heed his command.

Ashraf—at least she assumed he was the cleric she sought—sat on a cushion, waiting in silence. He had lighted another lamp. She could see him more clearly now, and it was his eyes that commanded her attention. They were young and alive, yet locked in a face that might have been moldering in the grave. But more than that, they were the eyes of a madman—wild and dangerous. For the first time since she was a small child, Badr was frightened.

"The stories are true," Ashraf said. "I possess charms that will thwart the power of demons. It is my calling, my purpose in life, to find and destroy the seed of Satan. You have timed well your visit, Princess, as I have just today returned from a successful venture. Now, pray, tell me how I can serve you."

Badr sensed that this man served no one, save perhaps Allah, and even then she suspected it was on his own terms. "I have been wronged by one of your 'seeds of Satan,' and I seek revenge," she said. "A demon. A jinni hidden in a battered oil lamp."

The cleric's eyes burned brighter at the word *jinni*. Encouraged, the Princess launched into her story, skillfully recasting the truth. She ignored Aladdin's ownership of the lamp as she told of the guttersnipe who had scaled the walls of the palace and invaded the sanctity of her suite. "Though how the beggar girl managed to evade the guards is still a mystery, and how she knew of the lamp's magic a greater mystery still."

The cleric's wild gaze focused for the first time on Badr's face, his eyes narrowing. "You possessed the lamp? You dabbled in the cruel enchantments of demon spawn?"

"No, no," Badr replied in haste. "That is the mystery, you see. I had no knowledge of the lamp's power. So how did this waif know? And how did she know it was in my hands?"

"Perhaps this . . . waif . . . is more than she seems. A sorceress, perhaps?"

"It could be so," Badr agreed. "Dare you challenge such a one?"

Ashraf laughed—a low, guttural sound—as the folds in his ancient face puckered with disdain.

"A stupid question," she said. "Forgive me."

The cleric's fingers moved in a quick curling motion—a signal for Badr to continue her tale.

"I couldn't let the theft go unpunished. What sort of message would that send to the villains of Al-Kal'as? So I eventually tracked the girl to her lair.

"When I—and my guards—tried to wrest the lamp from her, she brushed it with her fingers. The most loathsome demon roared from the spout, and then . . ." Badr paused, a well-timed tear trickling down her cheek. She could see that her description of calling forth the jinni (borrowed from Aladdin) had rung true to the cleric.

"Fact is, I simply don't remember what happened next," she continued. "I lay near death for some days, my men tell me. They fared little better. When we, by the hand of Allah, finally recovered, we found ourselves a thousand leagues from home. We were in the desert not far from Makkah. I am certain Aminah, for that is the sorceress's name, has counted us dead. I must rid the world of this evil thing—this demon jinni. Will you help me?"

Ashraf sat for a moment, still as death. At last he nodded. "I will help you."

The Full Moon of Full Moons smiled with stunning lunar radiance, though it seemed to have little effect on the cleric. "I do wish to be there when you do it," she said. "I desire to see the demon perish."

"I understand," said Ashraf. "And now, though I find it distasteful to bring up the subject of money, we must discuss the terms. Regrettably, payment for my services is necessary in order to continue my work."

"Will ten thousand dinars suffice?" Badr asked.

Ashraf almost smiled as he nodded. "We must depart this very night, before the trail grows yet colder," he said. "Bring in your man, the one who spoke from the darkness, for I will need him to carry my things."

Badr hurried down the stairs and struggled to unlock the door. Saladin pushed his way inside the moment the bolt came free. Silencing his questions, she led him to Ashraf.

They found the cleric loading a crate with his belongings. He ignored them as he worked, and they looked on without disturbing him. Besides a meager wardrobe, Ashraf added a strange assortment of bottles, vials, parchments, and charms to the crate, including a lidded coffer fashioned from an unidentifiable substance. Badr noticed that the cleric took special care to secure the unusual box, wrapping it carefully in layers of cloth.

"What is that?" asked Saladin, daring to break the silence. He pointed to the padded bundle Ashraf had just placed within the crate.

"There is a matter for which I will need your help," Ashraf said to Badr, ignoring the Captain of the Guard. Saladin stiffened, and the Princess placed a calming hand on his arm. "I tell you now so that you may be thinking of how to accomplish the task. I will need you to help me find something belonging to this witch, Aminah—a garment, some other possession, or, of most worth, a hair from her head. No, do not ask me why. It is a secret I shall not yet reveal."

"I will do as you ask, of course," said Badr. "I doubt very much that Aminah still dwells in Al-Kal'as, but perhaps we will find something left behind in her house. Here, take this. It is but a small part of the payment. I will pay you half the full amount when we reach Al-Kal'as—the balance when the task is complete."

The cleric bowed to the Princess. "Let the journey begin," he said, motioning for Saladin to take his crate.

three

WHEN AMINAH AND JINNI finally arrived on the terrace, their supper was cold. "I fear it's ruined," Barra lamented.

"Ah, not so, my dear," said Jinni, dropping to one knee before her. "I shall reconstitute and reheat every delectable bite." He glanced at Aminah. "No wish required, of course."

Hassan snorted. "Only because you'd rather that fish fried in vinegar and sesame oil be searing hot when you eat it."

"And I do not like congealed butter on tepid rice, either," the demon added with a broad grin. His sharp smile stretched the full circumference of his plum-colored head. Hassan winced at the sight.

Mouth snapping back into place, Jinni lifted the cover from

the platter of fried fish. He glared at it, along with the other dishes laid out before him.

"Ow!" cried Hassan. The fish had begun to sizzle, spitting hot oil and scorching the back of his hand.

"Take care uncovering the rice," said Jinni as Aminah reached for the covered bowl. "I may have applied a bit more heat than needed." The lid rattled as if the contents were boiling, and she pulled her hand away.

"Magic," said Hassan. "You can't rely on it."

Jinni turned a sour eye on him, but before he could retort, Aminah stood and began pouring iced sherbet for everyone. Though it was watered down from sitting so long, no one complained.

As they sipped their drinks, the night breezes caressed and soothed them, as well as cooling their fare. Soon Barra was serving the meal, and as they ate, happy conversation mingled with the whispering of the surf.

Afterward, they all pitched in to help Barra remove the platters and bowls. Each night when the terrace was clear, chess and backgammon boards usually appeared, but this time they chose to spend the evening gazing at the moonlit sea and talking quietly. Before long, they were sitting in comfortable silence, lost in their own thoughts.

Finally, Aminah stood. She leaned over to plant a quick kiss on the cheeks of Barra and Jinni. Then she embraced Hassan, brushing his lips with hers, and said good night. The others followed her to the bottom of the stairs and then wandered off in their separate directions—except for Jinni, who vaporized into a lavender cloud that drifted toward the lamp.

Aminah trailed behind the demon mist and watched it seep through the space beneath her apartment door. She reached the lamp as the last of Jinni's essence flowed lazily down its spout, and without waiting for him to settle in, she rubbed the brass surface with her sleeve, summoning him out again.

Instead of a light mist this time, plum-colored smoke curled from the lamp. A purple form materialized within the vapors, sliding from the spout and lying inert on the floor. As Jinni's features crystallized, Aminah could see he was asleep and snoring gently.

She was surprised to discover that demons slept—and that Jinni had managed it so quickly. But more surprising yet were Jinni's nightclothes—an odd top and bottom, both white and covered with circles outlined in blue. The center of each circle was also white, except for a red shape like a crescent moon. She nudged Jinni with her toe, and he shot to his feet with a yelp, turning a deeper shade of purple.

"What are you wearing?" she asked. "You look ridiculous."

"Nothing!" he snapped.

"If it were nothing, then you'd be naked. Oh, my, now that's an awful thought."

Jinni scowled.

"And what are those strange markings?" Aminah reached out to trace one of the circles. Jinni slapped away her hand.

"Excuse me while I change into something less comfortable," he said, preparing to snap his fingers.

"Wait! This is about the future again, isn't it? The same sort of strange things you've mentioned before—pizza, motion pictures, New York City."

Jinni rubbed his eyes and stretched. His skin lightened, and he seemed less cranky. "It is the symbol representing a sport team called the Cubs—yes, in the far distant future."

Aminah looked puzzled.

"A collection of men who play a game for money," he said, impatient again. "People pay to watch."

"Pay to watch grown men play a game? You're joking, aren't you?" said Aminah. "People aren't that stupid. Now, if they were racing stallions, or—"

"Do you wish to know about this sport or not?" Jinni raised his chin indignantly.

Aminah nodded. "But let me make it clear, I am *not* wishing to know. This is *not* a wish."

"Yes, yes," he grumbled, rolling his eyes. They popped from their sockets, spinning several circles about his head, then snapped back into place before he continued. "These men hit a ball with a stick and run around in a field. The object is to— oh, it is too difficult to explain."

"Let me understand this," said Aminah. "People pay money to watch men hit a ball with a stick. And run about in a field."

"Laugh if you must."

"You enjoy this game so much that you dress in the players' clothing?" Aminah asked.

Jinni smiled, showing rows of pointed teeth. "And I like the hot dogs and peanuts even more."

"The what?"

"Food! Spectators at the game devour them by the cartload."

Aminah groaned. "How can you think of food when your stomach is bulging?"

"Ah," was Jinni's only answer as he ran his tongue across his lips.

"I'd like to make my second wish for Ella," said Aminah. "Can you perform your magic dressed like that?"

"I would rather not. Allow me a moment to change from these pajam—ah, this uniform." Jinni's complexion deepened once again as he snapped his fingers. In an instant, he was a purple blur, twirling at a dizzying speed. Then just as quickly, he came to a stop. Bare-chested but clad in billowing pants, Jinni wore shoes with sharp, curling toes and a turban of violet silk. The demon shot upward to twice his height, his head ricocheting off the ceiling. "Yow! By Azráeel, that hurt!"

"I didn't think jinn felt real pain," said Aminah, surprised yet again.

"This is the price I must pay for the vast amounts of human food you force on me," he answered, returning to normal height.

"Yes." Aminah laughed. "It's a terrible challenge to make you eat."

"However, make no mistake. I would not change a thing," Jinni said. "You know, I have never tasted a hot dog or a peanut, because no human ever offered. But I could take you to the city of Chicago, where the Cubs play their game, and you then could purchase them for me."

"Oh, may I?" At her sarcasm, Jinni's face fell, and Aminah quickly recanted. "No, I'd really like to see your game—and taste peanuts. But first we must finish with Ella."

At this, Jinni bowed and said, "Ask whatso thou wishest. I am the slave between thy hands, oh noble one."

"Ella needs a persuasive tongue—a golden tongue, so to speak. If she is to make a difference, I fear she'll have to convince Prince Louis to do the right things. That's my second wish for her."

"Not as flashy as a crystal slipper," said Jinni, raising his arms, "but nevertheless, it is done."

Aminah was caught off guard by the demon's simple words. Usually, he was far more dramatic in his wish granting, resorting to grand gestures, loud noises, and long, formal phrases. In an instant he had given the wish and, as was customary, had disappeared back into the lamp.

"That deserves a hot dog," Aminah said to the empty room.

She replaced the lamp on the shelf of the closet and took up the scrying orb with the thought of peering in on Ella. The glass globe began to radiate its usual warmth, but then it quickly became blistering. Aminah dropped the glass onto its golden stand just before her fingers were singed. Then, instead of the orb's cheerful voice echoing in her head, there came the foreign sound of rumbling thunder. Within, its typical curls of scarlet mist had given way to dark thunderheads—burgundy in color and punctuated by brilliant crimson flashes.

Alarmed by behavior she'd never before seen from the orb, Aminah stepped back. The globe, battered as the storm inside erupted, began rocking back and forth perilously.

Then, as if the tempest had only been meant to get her attention, the orb cleared. Gazing into its depths, Aminah saw the drawing room of the house where Ella lived.

Moonlight dusted the room with silver. Two figures emerged from the shadows and floated forward, their long white dressing gowns whispering in the dark. They stopped at a window, where the moon revealed two rather unremarkable female faces. Aminah recognized them instantly—Ella's stepsisters. That these lazy louts were sacrificing sleep could only mean trouble.

The taller of the two reached out to unlatch a window, but her sister laid a hand on her arm. "Sophronia, I'm frightened," said the shorter girl, her voice quavering.

"You're such a child, Marie," Sophronia answered with a sneer, shaking her sister's fingers from her sleeve. The window's lead mullions sliced the silvery light into diamond shapes that crisscrossed her sour expression.

"But are we certain—really, truly certain—that the mysterious stranger dancing with Prince Louis was Ella? Her mask made it impossible to tell."

"Oh, please! You know it was Ella as well as I do. You're just a coward, that's all. But I'm brave enough to see that the little trollop doesn't attend the third ball. She won't be around for Prince Louis to choose as his bride."

"But you will," said Marie, brightening at the thought. "And we'll live in the palace and have servants and eat cake every single day."

"You'd be as sorry as I if Ella married the Prince. We'd be left to live like . . . like this." She pointed at the ample contents of the drawing room. "That's why what we're doing is worth the risk." She flipped open the latch.

Marie stifled a terrified squeal as a gloved hand eased the glass open. An arm snaked over the window ledge, trailed by a form wrapped in black. The man stood in silence, waiting, until Sophronia spoke.

"The girl's in the cellar," she said. Her voice had an edge as sharp and hard as flint. "Follow me."

Sophronia led him to a door, behind which a steep stairway plunged into the darkness. "Her room is at the end of the corridor. Remember, she must not attend tomorrow night's Royal Ball. In fact, she must not show her face to the Prince—not ever again."

"But don't hurt her," whimpered Marie.

Sophronia pursed her lips, considering her sister's plea. "I suppose you shouldn't do her any real harm," she said at last.

The dark man nodded and held out a gloved hand. Sophronia sighed, reaching into the folds of her robe, and dropped a leather purse bulging with coins into his fingers. "The second half at the next full moon," she said. "We must be certain the cellar room remains empty."

He nodded again, tucking the bag of coins into the lining of his cloak. From the same deep pocket he extracted a length of cord to bind Ella, and then slipped soundlessly down the cellar stairs. Once out of sight, he exchanged the rope for a long, narrow-bladed dagger.

Aminah leapt back from the orb as if she'd been struck. She swept up her thawb and threw it on. The robe shivered as it settled on her shoulders, and threatening images of long knives and blood-drenched scimitars began to stab and hack their way across its surface.

With no thought of summoning Jinni, Aminah closed her eyes, calling on magic from one of her earliest wishes—the ability to travel across any distance and through time. It was the way she attended to Ahab and Ella and the others chosen by the orb.

Aminah envisioned Ella's cramped cellar bedroom, and

braced herself for the icy blast that came with a leap across space and time. Her skin prickled, and the hair on her arms and neck stood on end just before a dizzying jerk pulled her from the room.

The soft sound of her feet touching down on a stone floor was the only hint that she'd arrived. Windowless, Ella's room was sloe-black, but Aminah willed the thawb to quell its usual glow. As if it were holding its breath, the robe lay dormant.

Certain she'd landed precisely on the spot she'd pictured in her mind's eye, Aminah nevertheless reached out in the darkness to confirm her location—and to steady herself. Traveling through time always upset her stomach, and she fought to keep down her supper.

She stood between the damp foundation wall and the girl's bedstead, and as the nausea left her, Aminah heard Ella purring in her sleep. Then the air in the room stirred; the door had swung open without a sound. *Sophronia oiled the hinges,* Aminah thought as she sidestepped the bed frame and repositioned herself between Ella and the intruder.

The villain must have caught the sound of her movements, for his muffled footfalls stopped. Aminah sensed they stood face-to-face, and a moment later his tentative hand brushed her arm.

How he managed to stifle an outcry, Aminah didn't know, but she admired his cool control. She heard him take a backward step, and before he could make his next move, Aminah pounced.

A blinding explosion of light sent the dark figure to his knees. Squinting against the brilliance, he looked up—and screamed. A flaming figure rose before him, a terrible hag draped in a burning robe. Blazing fingers of fire reached out-ward, threatening to draw him into the conflagration.

He screamed again as fiery beasts leapt from the hag's robe, their frenzied snarling battering his ears. Blood and gore dripped from rows of serrated fangs. Insane with bloodlust, they strained to reach his throat, barely contained by the garment's glowing weave. These creatures exceeded the man's worst nightmares, and, overcome with fear, he was rooted in place.

"Flee!" the burning crone shrieked. "Flee, if you value life!"

Frozen still, the man cowered, until one of the beasts almost broke free. At the heat of its fetid breath on his cheek, he found his legs and bolted from the room.

Once he'd cleared the doorway, the room fell silent. The inferno licking about Aminah died, leaving the robe pulsing with a warm glow that still lit the room.

A girl, whose pleasant features were etched with fear, peeked from behind the straw-filled bedstead. She stood on wobbly legs and whispered, "He had a knife."

Aminah sat heavily on the edge of the bed and gave herself a moment to recover before turning to the wide-eyed girl. "I hope he only meant to frighten you, Ella," she said.

"No, I think he meant to use it. You saved my life," said Ella. "Does Sophronia hate me so much?"

Aminah shook her head. "She only wanted him to take you away. I suppose the rogue may have had other ideas."

Shaking, Ella sat down on the bed. "You can be quite fright-ening, too. Is that proper for a fairy godmother?"

"Quite proper, Ella. I assure you," she answered with a weak smile. For a moment, the voice that matched her elderly vis-age gave way, and a youthful sound escaped.

Ella peered into the old woman's lively eyes. "You *are* a mystery," she said. "Are you old or young—I'm never quite certain."

"It's the way of things with fairy godmothers," said Aminah.

The girl crawled across the bed and embraced her. "Well, that question was quite daring of me," she said. "Is one allowed to hug fairies?"

Aminah laughed, the creases in her ancient face folding in on themselves. "Yes—at least when we aren't on fire. Now, Ella, you must listen. Sophronia will keep you from the third ball if you stay in this house. Come, there's a place not far from here where you'll be safe."

four

"I HID ELLA WITH THE MILLER—she and his daughter have long been secret friends," said Aminah, several days later. "She'll be safe there until we can get her to the third ball, but we must to do something more to protect the girl. Any ideas?"

Jinni's hand mechanically fed sweetmeats into his purple face as he and Hassan stared in fierce concentration at Aminah's chessboard. "Your move, demon," Hassan growled.

"Demon, eh?" Crumbs spewed from Jinni's mouth. "Name-calling—this means you smell defeat. But your pitiful attempt to distract me is useless."

"We'll see. You're not as wily as you believe, bottle imp."

"Bottle imp! Why, you impertinent—"

"Enough!" Aminah reached forward, shaking the low table and rattling the chessmen.

"No!" the two cried in unison.

Aminah might have laughed at the comic horror on their faces, but their bickering had begun to irritate her. "Am I watching two jackals snarling at each other over the same carcass? Try being civilized."

"No need." Jinni grinned as he slid an elephant-shaped playing piece across the board. "*Shah mat!* My *Fil* captures your *Shah*. The game is ended. Not bad for a bottle imp, eh?"

"Trickery!" Hassan cried, his cheeks scarlet. But then he sighed, leaning back on his cushion. "I suppose I deserved that," he said with a rueful laugh.

"A crushing loss!" Showers of celebratory violet sparks erupted from Jinni's ears, but his face sagged in disappointment when Hassan only nodded in agreement.

"Actually, you played well, my boy," Jinni said.

"Praise be to Allah!" Aminah exclaimed. "You can be civil."

Jinni floated into the air above his cushion, and then dropped his feet to the floor. "I've had enough of civility for one day—it weakens me. I'm off to the kitchen to regain my strength."

"But what about Ella? You're not leaving until I get an answer."

"Oh, let him go," said Hassan. "Besides, he tells me he thinks better on a full stomach."

"This is true, oh wise and generous Master. Then I shall ponder your question with a mind revitalized."

"Go," she said, waving him away. "Separating my two spitting jackals may be for the best."

As Jinni disappeared, Hassan said, "Good riddance."

Aminah sighed. "I think you enjoy scratching at each other."

He smiled. "I know I do."

"What should I do about Ella?" Aminah asked. "If her own stepsister wants her kidnapped, think about her life as a commoner who will rule as queen. She'll have an enemy at every turn."

"You have a wish left, right?"

"Yes," she answered.

"Then give her invulnerability," he said. "Jinni can do that, can't he?"

Stunned by Hassan's straightforward solution, Aminah could only stare. When she didn't say anything, Hassan awkwardly cleared his throat. "A dim-witted suggestion," he said. "Sorry."

"No, it's perfect! I was making this too difficult, imagining a host of invisible guardians and the like."

"Well, now," Hassan said with a chuckle. "One would expect the proper idea from an imaginative fellow like Idris, being a storyteller, but from a baker?"

"Not a surprise at all. You happen to be the most insightful baker in the entire caliphate. Even Idris would agree."

"I'm flattered," said Hassan. "However, I doubt he has time to think of us these days. Building a master storyteller's reputation must take every waking moment. That and fighting off the Caliph's dancing girls."

"Do I detect a hint of envy?"

"What? Why would I care for dancing girls when I have you?"

"You really are quite insightful—for a baker," said Aminah, delight dancing in her eyes.

They turned at the sound of sandals slapping the paving stones, and a moment later, Barra stood breathless in the open doorway. She stared at Aminah with shining eyes. "He's come home," she said, her voice breaking.

Aminah knew Barra's words could have only one meaning. Breathless now herself, she hurried past Barra and peered into the courtyard. "Idris!" she cried, running across the courtyard and throwing herself into his arms.

"Watch where you put those hands, storyteller," Hassan called. He stood a few paces back, grinning.

Idris extricated himself from Aminah's grasp, kissing her on the cheek.

"Watch where you put those lips!" cried Hassan, in mock horror. He rushed to Idris and crushed him in a mighty embrace. "It's good to see you, my friend, but none of us expected it would be so soon. And just as we were talking of you."

"Talking of me? Should I be worried?" Smiling, Idris let the saddlebags in his grasp slip to the ground. "No, you're right— when we parted in Al-Kal'as I didn't plan on seeing you for ages. I suppose I should have saved myself the dust and sweltering heat and come with you by jinni magic in the first place."

"Yes, I suppose magic has its benefits," said Hassan, his eyes wandering to Aminah.

"Homesick for my cooking, no doubt," said Barra. She also embraced the young storyteller, then held him at arm's length. "Skinny as a stick. Well, we'll soon remedy that."

"Dear Barra." He kissed her on both cheeks. "Now that you mention it, I am famished."

"Our Alliance of the Lamp—all together again," said Aminah softly.

"What's that you say?" asked Idris.

"Our Alliance of the Lamp. That's what I call the five of us who survived Badr's wrath. Now come along." She hooked her arm in his and pulled him toward the kitchen. "This demands a celebration! Wait until you taste Hassan's cream puffs!"

"Another of his magical pastries?"

"My best effort," said Hassan. "A perfect delicacy for weddings."

"Is that an announcement?" asked Idris.

"Not yet," he answered. "We were waiting for you to resurface—so we could let you know when to show up for the ceremony. After all, we're still hiding from the Princess, so that limits the number of guests to invite. You make up a full one-third of our list, and that's counting the bottle imp. Now that the wind's blown you our way, we'll be setting our plans!"

Aminah laced her other arm through Hassan's. "Idris, you've just made a marriage," she said.

A juicy symphony of eating noises greeted them as they reached the cookery. Moans of ecstasy emanated from a figure hunched over a vast tray of various delicacies. He looked up at the faces crowded around him and smiled, a mouthful of well-chewed food dropping to the floor. "Ah, Idris, my boy! What a pleasant surprise."

"Hello, Jinni. That's a splendid tint of violet you're wearing today."

Jinni laughed, his skin suddenly striped in rainbow colors. "My, my, witty as ever," he said.

The others sat about, watching Idris and Jinni eat, but after nibbling on a few tidbits, Idris suddenly remembered his horses. "The same two stallions you gave me when I left Al-Kal'as," he said. "I must get them stabled."

"Then have Aminah show you to your quarters," said Barra. "You need to wash—and rest. I'll ready a meal fit for a master storyteller. We'll join on the terrace when the day cools."

"Mother Barra, how I've missed you," said Idris.

❂

EVEN THOUGH THE SUN HAD SET, the walls of Aminah's estate and the paving blocks of her courtyard radiated the day's heat like an oven. But in the midst of a desert of blistering stone, the terrace was an oasis cooled by the sea.

Barra, with Jinni's help, prepared nothing short of a feast to honor Idris's surprise visit. Aminah allowed the demon to assume the human visage of Uncle Omar for their reunion celebration. After all, it was the only way Jinni had appeared to the others back in Al-Kal'as, when Aminah was keeping the demon a secret from everyone.

Together, Barra and Jinni ferried trays and bowls from kitchen to terrace, and as Barra was lighting the lanterns, the rest of the Alliance of the Lamp gathered on the twilit rooftop. With Hassan on one side of her and Idris on the other, Aminah couldn't have been happier.

"Do you still have your bakery, Hassan?" Idris asked after they had all served themselves.

"Yes," Aminah answered for him. "And he still has Jinni's gifts with flour and milk, as well as the magic ovens and jars."

"I inquired about your bakeshop in Tyre, but no one knew of you."

"Aminah's wisdom," Hassan answered. "She counseled me from the beginning to use another name, so I chose Ibrahim."

"Are you still giving away your bread?" Idris asked. "If a hungry mob is constantly at your door, I fear word will eventually find its way to the Princess."

"What are you saying, Idris?" asked Aminah, puzzled. "That feeding the poor isn't worth the risk?"

"Not too much of a risk," he answered. "Badr is probably back in Al-Kal'as by now. She'll be on the hunt again, and as you know, her resources are formidable. Spies will be in every city."

"Yes, we've thought of that," said Hassan. "Therefore, I devised a way to distribute the bread at locations away from the bakery. It is moved at night, in secrecy."

"That's good," said Idris.

"Do you know something more of Badr?" asked Aminah, uneasy at the relief in his voice. "Is that why you are asking these questions?"

"No, no. She frightens me, that's all. And as I said, I don't think you can be too cautious. But enough! I was a fool to speak her name—the mere mention of which threatens to poison our evening. Tell me instead what you and Jinni have been doing. Have you come to the aid of any more Ahabs or Hassans? I assume you still use the lamp for good purposes."

Uncle Omar grunted, waving a chicken leg in the air to get Idris's attention. Everyone waited until he'd swallowed a gargantuan mouthful. "This last effort is shaping up as my best work!" he exclaimed.

Barra giggled, and glancing at her, he grumbled, "Aminah's best work, I mean. We jinn loathe good deeds, you remember."

"Yes, I remember—though I must say you seem quite enthusiastic about this latest project. Tell me what you've accomplished thus far," Idris urged.

"I will do better than that," said Uncle Omar, perking up. He dropped the chicken bone and began to spin like a whirlwind. When he stopped, the image of Ella stood on the terrace.

They passed the next hour barely able to breathe for the laughter as Jinni took every part in Ella's story, dividing himself into several characters at once. The most popular scene was Ella's rescue from sure death at the hands of the dark scoundrel. Jinni's rendition of the man's screams and the snarling thawb surprised even Aminah. But when he recreated the villain's mad dash up the cellar stairs and his leap through the glass of a closed window, everyone cheered—especially Aminah, who was seeing this for the first time herself. When the performance ended, Hassan begged him to do it again.

"I thought you didn't like magic," Aminah whispered in his ear.

He grinned. "I'll make an allowance this once."

During Jinni's second performance, Aminah glanced several times in Idris's direction. Though he laughed along with the rest of them, he seemed distracted. He fidgeted, tapping his foot and cracking his knuckles, and kept peering into the darkness as though he were watching for something. Then just as the blackheart was about to dive through the window,

Idris's attention wandered again, and the loud shattering of glass startled him. His hand flew upward, and the sherbet in his glass drenched his tunic.

"What a clumsy fool!" he cried, leaping to his feet. "I'm sorry, Jinni . . . Uncle Omar. I've interrupted your tale."

"You're soaked," said Aminah, dabbing at his shirt with a serving cloth. "I think you'd better change."

"Yes, though it may take a while to find something suitable in my pack. Carry on, Uncle Omar. I promise to sneak back without a sound."

Hassan insisted on a third performance, and Aminah noticed Idris didn't return until it was almost finished. Afterward, they stretched out on their carpets, leaning against pillows and gazing at the stars.

"So, Uncle Omar," said Idris, "do you live outside the lamp these days?"

"Not entirely. Aminah and I decided it is better not to stray so far from my true nature. I will return to the lamp tonight—after I have eaten my fill," he said, taking up a bowl of dates.

"In that case, you may never return," said Hassan.

"Ah, baker's humor." Jinni's mouth stretched to accommodate the bowl's entire contents, forcing Barra to look away.

"I've always wondered how you find the lamp," Idris continued. "I mean, if it's been moved while you're outside it."

"What a strange question," said Aminah. "You weren't a bit interested in such things when we were in Al-Kal'as."

"Storytelling has made me curious, I suppose," he answered. "You're right, it's a silly question. Something that just popped into my head."

Jinni wiped his mouth with the back of his hand and swallowed the enormous lump of half-chewed dates. "Not so silly, my boy. Fascinating, I would say, and the answer is, 'I do not know.'"

Barra rose and began collecting empty platters. "Oh, leave them, Barra. I'll help you later," said Aminah. Then she turned to Jinni and asked, "What do you mean, you don't know?"

"It simply happens. Say you have taken the lamp into Tyre, and I am in the stable. If I had a sudden desire to be inside the lamp, I would be. And the same would happen whether someone had dropped it to the bottom of the sea or an eagle had lifted it to the top of a mountain."

"Bottom of the sea! That would be a damp surprise," said Idris.

"The lamp does not leak. I settled onto a riverbed once and did not know. I appear inside without a clue as to where the lamp is. But of course, there was seldom an occasion when it was out of my sight—until now, that is. Mostly I would appear, grant a wish, and then—as I was in the lamp's presence—return at my own speed and in a manner of my choosing."

"With a puff of lavender smoke, for instance," said Aminah. "But what about when you forget to think small as you're sliding into the lamp? He forgot once, you know, and it wasn't a pretty sight. I called him back right away, but you should have seen him! All charred and—"

"Enough!" cried Jinni. "This is Idris's night, so I suggest we hear from our traveling storyteller."

"But he is a true professional," said Hassan, his face sagging with exaggerated sorrow. "I doubt we have the gold to coax a tale from him."

Idris laughed. "There isn't gold enough in a sultan's treasure hoard—at least, not for you, Hassan. However, the rest of these fine people deserve a tale at no charge. Come, gather around, and if Hassan happens to overhear, there is nothing to be done about it."

Five

THEY PULLED CUSHIONS NEAR IDRIS, whose jovial manner had turned serious. "I have traveled far today and am weary. Forgive me if I have the strength only for a short tale—short but laden with meaning. Listen carefully, my children, to the tale of 'The Ruined Man Who Became Rich Again.'"

There lived once in Baghdad a wealthy man, who then lost a great deal of his substance when thieves attacked the caravan that carried his wares to market. And if that were not enough, a raging fire consumed his storehouse, leaving him so destitute that he could earn his living only by hard labor. One night, he lay down to sleep, dejected and heavyhearted, and saw in a dream a Speaker who said to him: "Thy fortune is in the land of Egypt, in the great city of Cairo. Go there and seek it."

So the man left his labors and set out for Cairo, but when he arrived in the great city, the evening overtook him. Therefore, he lay down to sleep in a mosque. Presently, a band of thieves entered the mosque and then made their way into an adjoining house. But the owners, being aroused by the noise of the bandits, awoke and cried out, whereupon the Chief of Police came to their aid with his officers.

The robbers made off, but the officers entered the mosque and, finding the man from Baghdad asleep there, laid hold of him and beat him with palm rods—so grievous a beating that he was well-nigh dead. Then they cast him in jail, where he stayed three days, after which the Chief of Police sent for him and asked him, "Whence do you come?"

"From Baghdad," he answered.

Said the Chief, "And what brought you to Cairo?"

"I saw in a dream One who said to me, 'Your fortune is in Cairo. Go there to it,'" said the Baghdadi. "But when I came to Cairo the fortune which he promised me proved to be the palm rods you so generously gave to me."

The Chief of Police laughed till he showed his wisdom teeth and said, "Oh, man of little wit, thrice have I seen in a dream one who said to me: 'There is in Baghdad a house in such a district and of such a fashion and its courtyard is laid out garden-wise, at the lower end whereof is a jetting fountain and under the same a great sum of money lies buried. Go there and take it.' Yet I went not; but you, due to the briefness of your wit, have journeyed from place to place, on the faith of a dream, which was but the idle nonsense of sleep."

Then the Chief gave the man from Baghdad money, say-
ing, "Take yourself herewith back to your own country."

The poor man accepted the money and set out upon his
homeward march.

Now, the house the Chief of Police had described was the
man's own house in Baghdad; so the wayfarer returned there
and, digging underneath the fountain in his garden, discovered
a great treasure. And thus Allah gave him abundant fortune.

Idris paused, gazing into Aminah's dark eyes. The music—the
magic—of his voice had mesmerized her, and she was barely
aware of his knowing look. Then he continued.

Remember this, my children, though it seems you have been
betrayed by one whom you trusted without doubt—as it
seemed the Baghdadi was betrayed by his dream—do not lose
faith. Hold to the belief and exercise patience, and all shall be
put to rights. All shall be to your benefit.

Idris stood and began gathering the plates and glasses. It
took a moment for the rest of the Alliance to stir. Without
speaking, they cleaned away the remnants of their feast.

"Off to my lamp," Jinni said when the work was done, and
in a vivid flash of lavender light, he vanished. Then the rest of
them, with wishes all around for pleasant dreams, separated to
their quarters.

◑

AMINAH CURLED UP ON HER BED amid pillows and a scattering of her father's old books. She'd selected one on astron-

omy, a subject that intrigued her, and yet the tome had lain open to the same star map for nearly an hour.

She stared at the swaying palm fronds outside her window, wondering about Idris. Though Aminah was overjoyed to see her friend, there was something unsettling about him. He'd seemed distant, almost disconnected, during their time together on the terrace. And his questions had been so unlike the things Idris would typically ask. But most of all, it was his tale that bothered her. Though sounding quite innocent, it had cast an ominous shadow over her. When Idris paused, peering deeply into Aminah's eyes, the story had suddenly become a hidden message meant for her alone. But if this were true, its meaning eluded her.

Aminah shrugged. "I'm being silly," she said aloud, closing her book and reaching for the scrying orb. Planning to check on Ella before falling asleep, she had taken the globe to bed with her, and now she lifted it from its nest among the pillows. The moment her fingers touched the glass, a cheery explosion of fiery pinwheels filled the orb and a haunting tune echoed in her ear.

"I wish to look in on Ella," she said. "But let's start with Ahab and Khalidah."

The crystal cleared, and Aminah could see the Baghdad street in front of the tailor's shop, which had been relocated to a spacious new building. At that moment, Ahab and Kalidah rounded a corner. Khalidah was holding the hand of a tiny figure—a girl so thin her great, brown doe eyes seemed too large for her face. The child chewed greedily on the end of a loaf of bread.

"You shall never be hungry again," Ahab said, with a broad

smile. "And you'll never be lonely again, either—now you have one hundred three brothers and sisters!"

"Did you hear that? One hundred three children!" said Aminah.

No, one hundred four, murmured a voice in her head.

Aminah smiled. "You're right," she said to the orb. "One hundred four."

She pulled the sphere closer as the scene shifted to the shop's interior, but as an exuberant throng of children rushed to meet their new sister, the image vanished. Aminah cried out as searing pain burned behind her eyes, and she dropped the orb.

Once the pain receded, Aminah took up the sphere, now cold and black. Mystified, she gazed at her rounded reflection staring back from its dark surface. For the second time in days, she held an orb that seemed unfamiliar—that had never until now shown her this side of itself.

She tried to link directly to its consciousness. This way of working the sphere sent images to her head rather than to the glass, and though this method made things more vivid—far more realistic—it always left her exhausted. Often she would sleep through the next day. Aminah hoped this stronger sort of connection would bridge whatever it was that had separated her from the magic crystal. But she found only unaccustomed darkness—a blank mindscape—behind her eyelids. When she looked at the orb again, it was choked with ugly clouds the color of soot.

Panic clutched Aminah's heart as she hurried to open the hidden closet. *Has something gone wrong with Ahab? Or Ella?* she wondered. She threw on her magic thawb, and then, motivated by fear, she locked the closet door and covered it with the sandalwood panel. Closing her eyes, Aminah concentrated on the paving stones outside Ahab's shop. She braced herself for the disorienting jerk that would take her to Baghdad. But no icy needles pricked her skin, and she opened her eyes, staring dumbly at the familiar walls of her room. It was then she noticed that the thawb was lifeless. No throbbing lights or dancing images. No wailing or whistling or snarling. She was clothed in nothing more than a commonplace robe.

"Jinni," she whispered, and ran to retrieve the lamp. She threw back the sandalwood panel, fumbling with the disks that unlocked the closet. But before she could get inside, the door to her apartment flew open, and she hurried toward it.

As she stepped into the next room, she froze. Aminah and Jinni stared at each other in stunned silence. Unable to believe her eyes, she circled him, not seeing the purple visage of a demon but rather the face of a younger Uncle Omar. No, not Omar. She drew in a surprised breath at the hardened features of Gindar.

Aminah had come face-to-face with Gindar only once before, when she'd traveled back in time to seek Jinni's forgotten roots. To her dismay, as well as Jinni's, she'd uncovered an unsavory truth—that he'd been a young man so overcome by greed, so filled with disdain for others, that he'd invited the life of a demon. Aminah had witnessed the terrible moment when the curse had taken Gindar, stripped him of his memories, and made him the unwilling servant of anyone who possessed the lamp.

"What are *you* doing here?" she asked.

"I wanted to sleep in a place with a window," mumbled

Gindar, "so I took one of the spare rooms. But then . . ." He looked about, his gaze disoriented.

Aminah realized with relief that his voice lacked Gindar's disdainful tone. "You were to sleep in the lamp," she said crossly. Then noticing his clouded eyes, she leaned closer. "Is something wrong?"

Gindar—or Jinni—shrugged. "I feel odd," he whispered.

"Perhaps if you were to return to the lamp," Aminah suggested.

"Yes, perhaps," he murmured, but he didn't disappear.

"Are you waiting for my permission? Well, you have it. Go!"

Gindar glanced away, and then turned back with an anguished look. "I cannot!"

"Yes, you can. I command you."

He shook his head. "I have not the power."

As Aminah gaped at the forlorn face, a chilling thought wormed its way into her mind. She left Gindar and crept, almost unwillingly, back to the closet. She twirled the tumblers and pulled on the iron door.

Aminah fell to her knees in the opening and sobbed. The shelf that held the lamp was bare. She hadn't noticed earlier, when she'd taken the orb.

To her shame, her thoughts flew to Idris—his detached behavior, his wandering eyes, his long absence from the terrace. And his sly behavior from days past, such as spying on her to learn the secret of the lamp. Rising on unsteady legs, she stumbled past Gindar, whose eyes were locked in a vacant stare.

The windows were dark when she reached Idris's room, but still she pounded on the door. The hammering echoed in the night air, and soon Hassan and Barra came scurrying into the courtyard.

"Bring a light," she called, and Hassan stepped back into his apartment, returning with an oil lantern. He hurried to her side, and they entered Idris's quarters together.

"He's gone," she said in a small voice. "And he's taken the lamp."

◗

"DON'T BLAME YOURSELF." Hassan's tone was meant to be soothing, but it only distressed Aminah all the more.

"How can you say that?" she wailed. "I made it easy for him. I was the one who instructed Jinni to make the hidden closet exactly the same as in Al-Kal'as. I was the one who used the identical combination of symbols to unlock the door, even though I realized Idris knew them."

"No one could have guessed he'd be a threat," said Barra. She glanced nervously at Jinni, who had begun wandering absently about Aminah's apartment.

"That's true," said Hassan. "There was no way to predict that—"

"Gold!" The cry came from the closet. "Piles and piles of it!"

Recognizing the change in Jinni's voice, Aminah stiffened. Though Hassan and Barra had never heard Gindar speak, they reacted to the unfamiliar sound. The three moved in unison toward the closet door. Peering into the tiny room, they found Jinni on his knees, his hands scooping gold coins from a great, glittering mound. He paused a second, turning to leer at them, and then began filling the deep pockets of his sarwal with his newfound treasure.

Aminah pulled Hassan and Barra aside. In hushed tones, she explained what she knew of Gindar, and as she did, a tiny whimper escaped Barra. She could see Omar in the young man's features, and yet this person was a stranger. The raging fire in his eyes frightened her. And his mouth, turned upward in an avaricious smirk, made a mockery of Omar's smile.

When Aminah finished her tale, she returned to Gindar. "Come out of my closet," she commanded. "But first, empty your pockets."

Startled, Gindar struggled under the weight of his load, scattering coins as he stood. Aminah didn't know if he would recognize her—perhaps none of Jinni remained—but his eyes narrowed at the sight of her.

"Your friend is still about, somewhere in here." With a sneer, Gindar rubbed his stomach. "However, I'll wager you've seen the last of him," he said, with a sharp bark of laughter.

"Come out of there. Now! We must talk," Aminah said, but she blocked the door until he reluctantly parted with every gold coin. Then she moved aside as he swaggered from the closet. Barra and Hassan backed away.

"So Idris stole your lamp," Gindar said. "Well, *I* never trusted the filthy little jackal, like the rest of you. He had shifty eyes, that one."

"Oh, shut up!" cried Barra. "Idris is a good boy. There must be some mistake—some misunderstanding." With pleading eyes, she looked at Aminah, who could tell that losing Idris and Omar at the same instant was almost more than Barra could bear.

"There's no mistake," said Hassan.

"No, Barra's right." Aminah stepped back to the closet. The

others followed, Gindar pushing his way to the front. "See all that gold?"

"May I touch it again?" asked Gindar, his stony eyes beginning to blaze.

Aminah ignored him and squeezed by Hassan, who guarded the way in. Once inside, she picked up the enchanted teakwood money box and unceremoniously dumped its coins on the floor.

"Just as I thought," she said, shaking the empty container. "It didn't replenish itself." Hassan stood aside so Barra and Gindar could see. "And my orb remains dark and unresponsive. All enchantments are gone from us. Idris knew this would happen, and so he emptied the chest over and over again before its magic ended—gold to tide us over."

"You sound as if he's planning to return with the lamp, but he isn't. No, the gold is naught but cushion for his conscience," said Gindar. "Let's face it, he wanted riches for himself, and the lamp will give him all that and more."

"He has no need for riches. I gave him a money box of his own," said Aminah. "Besides, the lamp won't help him without a jinni."

"That's right!" Hassan exclaimed. "You're not in the lamp, Jinni."

"I am *not* your jinni!" Gindar retorted. "And good riddance, I say, to that groveling donkey's rear. That despicable lump of demon trash—*ow!*"

Barra stepped back, shocked by her impetuous attack. Gindar rubbed his flaming cheek where she had struck him, but suddenly his face blanched. Groaning and holding his head, he folded onto a nearby diwan. When he looked up, though his stare was blank, Gindar's smirk was gone.

"What has happened to me?" he asked, and in spite of his piteous tone, Barra squealed in delight. She dropped down beside him and kissed his cheek. "Why, Barra!" Uncle Omar exclaimed.

"Where have you been hiding?" she asked, blushing.

"A better question might be, "Where is Gindar hiding?'" said Hassan. Then he nudged the closet door closed just enough to shield Aminah's gold from Omar's eyes.

six

I see by your eyes that you are wondering, did I steal A's lamp? Oh, yes, I took it! "But why?" you ask.

My motive for separating A from her magic arose as I made my way to Makkah in those earlier, happier days. A caravan passed, traveling in the opposite direction. Had I not looked up at just the right moment, I would have completed the pilgrimage. Instead, I raised my eyes and saw the Princess and her Captain of the Guard making their way home.

I must tell you, my heart was seized with fear at the sight of her. Then I noticed another man accompanying the Princess and her henchmen, and his countenance added to my sense of dread. Overcome by a foreboding pall, I circled back.

I am very good at spying. Through eavesdropping I had once

saved A from the Princess by learning the lamp's secret. I wouldn't hesitate to do it again. So after nightfall, I crept up to the Princess's tent, unbeknownst to her drunken guards. Through a peephole, I watched and listened, shuddering whenever the stranger with the Princess spoke. He was corpselike, and it truly seemed as if his words fell from the lips of the living dead.

From his own cadaverous mouth, I discovered him to be a rogue cleric—one who hunts and destroys demons. He was in the Princess's employ because he held the means to locate A's lamp and destroy her jinni.

Armed with this new and dreadful knowledge, I found the caravan chief and joined his train. It was fortunate he had room for another traveler. And it was fortunate that the Princess and her Captain had never before laid eyes on me.

I needed a way into the palace, if I wished to keep abreast of her plans, and so I made certain to impress the Princess with my prodigious storytelling abilities. While on the road, I shared many a tale in the nightglow of campfires, and thereby won her favor. Even a blackheart loves a good story.

When we neared the city of her birth, the Princess invited me to board in the palace and entertain her father. But when we arrived, she learned the Sultan was dead and her husband ruled in his place. It was no great surprise for the Princess. The old man had been teetering on the edge of life since before the jinni had whisked her away to Makkah. Nevertheless, it seemed clear to me that the loss deepened both her hatred for A and her need to possess the lamp. The girl who had shamed her in so many ways was now also the girl who had kept her from her father's deathbed.

But enough! Let me return to telling you more of A and her missing lamp.

"I WILL NOT BELIEVE Idris took the lamp for his own gain," said Aminah, her eyes damp.

Standing in the stable, she and the others had just confirmed what they'd already guessed: Idris's horses were gone. Hassan and Barra were still in the doorway, but Jinni stood with his arms about the neck of his favorite mount.

He's frightened. The horses are a comfort, Aminah thought, rocking back against the stable wall. She slid downward into the dirt, doubling over in misery. The sudden disconnect from her magic had left her with a gnawing pain that hollowed her insides. Barra started toward her, but Aminah pulled herself up and stumbled forward to join Jinni, pressing her cheek against the warm, pungent horseflesh.

"Hasn't Idris proven himself a loyal friend?" she asked, her voice muffled. "Remember, he took the lamp once before, but only to save us from Badr. And now he's done it again to protect us from some other danger."

"Then why didn't he confide in you?" Hassan asked. "Why didn't he trust you to understand?"

"I don't know!" Aminah cried. The horse shook its head at her outburst, nostrils flaring. She stepped back, raising her hands helplessly. "I don't know," she repeated, no longer able to hold back the tears. Hassan reached out, taking her into his arms.

"With the lamp gone, Ahab's and Ella's gifts have deserted them. Yours, as well," she said to Hassan.

"Yes," he answered. "I wouldn't have believed it, but I do feel a little empty inside."

Aminah crumpled in Hassan's embrace. The thought of Ahab's orphans turned out into the streets, of Ella vulnerable to another assassin, was a knife in her belly. And what of Hassan's beggars? "We must find Idris!" she cried.

"Can't Jinni send himself to the lamp?" asked Barra.

"I suppose so," said Hassan. "A bottle imp will return to his flask without fail—even if it's been cast into the sea. Isn't that so, Uncle Omar?"

Jinni grinned. "Yes! How silly of me not to remember."

"You've also forgotten that you tried returning to the lamp earlier," said Aminah. "You couldn't do it."

Jinni laughed. "No, you must be mistaken. Give me the command, and you will see."

"I don't think I'm your Master any longer, Jinni," she said. "So I can't order you about."

Jinni gazed into the air before answering. "Odd. I do not sense a new Master. You will have to suffice, I suppose. Go on, give me the command."

Aminah shrugged sadly. "Return to the lamp," she said.

With a knowing smile, he snapped his fingers, and then with a look of outrage, he snapped them again. "This cannot be!" Jinni cried, groping his face. "I remain! What fell magic is at work? Idris must be found, and this spell undone. He cannot have traveled far—I shall fly forth to find him."

Jinni leapt upward, like a bird taking to the air, then dropped to the stable floor with a bone-wrenching thump. He rolled in the dust until he lay at Aminah's feet. "I am without enchantments," he said miserably. "I fear I am now"—he paused, shuddering—"merely human."

In dejected silence, they started back to Aminah's apartment, where they planned to weigh their options. Along the way, Aminah was barely able to control the rising panic. It gripped her chest, her breaths coming fast and shallow, while the hollow pain wrenched at her midsection. To make things worse, Aminah envisioned Ella sprawled across her bed, a face blackened from poison. She tried but failed to dispel images of Ahab, dragged away from Kalidah and cast into debtors' prison. Why had Idris done this? *He, as much as any of us, understood the consequences,* she thought bitterly. *No matter the danger, he should have confided in me. Together we could have imagined a better way than this.*

For an instant, her faith in him wavered. Might he have had other, darker motives for stealing the lamp? Then she recalled the final words of Idris's tale:

> *Remember this, my children, though it seems you have been betrayed by one whom you trusted without doubt—as it seemed the Baghdadi was betrayed by his dream—do not lose faith. Hold to the belief and exercise patience, and all shall be put to rights. All shall be to your benefit.*

Aminah shook her head, as if to dislodge her mistrust. To doubt Idris now would be to break the final thread that kept her from tumbling into an abyss of despair. Still, a sense of helplessness threatened to overwhelm her. Feeling as vulnerable as a hen among foxes, Aminah resolved to act rather than wait a moment longer. It was the only way for her to stay in control.

"We'll go after Idris now," she said as they entered her quarters. "If he has drawn danger away from us, then it follows him. We can't sit here, hoping for his return—not even for a day or two."

"How will we find him?" asked Hassan. "We might well spend our days lengthening the distance between us, should we choose the wrong direction."

An uncontrollable flash of anger shot through Aminah. "Would you do nothing?" she cried. "What if we had delayed when Badr was torturing you? Said to ourselves, there's no way to help—"

Hassan's stricken look stopped her. Aminah cringed at her own words, yet fury still roiled inside. Confused, she clamped down on her tongue until she was settled enough to murmur, "I'm sorry."

"No, Aminah. You're right," said Hassan. "We'll leave right away. Barra, you should stay, in case Idris returns. Jinni ought to stay, as well."

Jinni, who was sprawled on the diwan, sat up, bristling. "The demon of the lamp must be there when you locate it. I am the one who will recognize the evil enchantment that has arrested my magic, not you. And I will know what must be done to counteract the spell."

"It's true," said Aminah. "Jinni has to be with us."

"But Barra mustn't stay here alone," Hassan said. "It isn't safe."

"Then we'll all go," said Aminah. "Gather your things. We'll meet back here in half an hour."

As the demon of the lamp had nothing to gather, Aminah asked Hassan to pick a few things from his wardrobe for

Omar. Left alone with Jinni, she ignored him as she packed her saddlebags. Then she started for the hidden closet to fill her money belt with gold.

Except for a crack, the iron door had been closed. Now it yawned open before her. Aminah stepped to the entrance and found Jinni on his knees again, worshipping the mound of gold. Even from behind, she could see the change in his posture.

"I'll find that miserable camel dropping!" Gindar mumbled to himself. "And then I shall have gold enough for a lifetime!"

"Jinni!"

Slowly, the hunched figure turned to face her. "That would be Gindar, my dear," he said, scowling. "Be assured, I meant *we* rather than *I*. Whether I like it or not, I need your help— even though I know where Idris is headed."

Aminah stared in stunned silence. "You know?" Her tone was biting. "You know, and you said nothing?"

"It had not occurred to me until this moment," he answered calmly. "It was a small thought I sensed from Idris during supper."

She glanced over her shoulder at the sound of movement, and Hassan stepped into the room. "Here's your bag, Omar," he said, tossing it to the floor. Barra came in behind him.

"He knows," said Aminah, her eyes locked on Gindar. "He knows where Idris is going."

Puzzled, they joined her at the closet door. Hassan groaned at the sight of Gindar's sour face. "Not again!" he grumbled.

"Yes, I'm back to stay this time," Gindar sneered. "And yes, I know where Idris went, but I don't think I'll tell. Not just yet."

"Oh, I think you will," said Hassan.

The malice in his voice startled Aminah. It was something she'd never heard from him before, and so she moved to bar his way into the closet. "Don't," she said. "Then he may never tell us."

"Smart girl," said Gindar. "However, it's clear none of you think much of me, so I've reconsidered. Your help would be useful, but I'm clearly a thorn in your collective feet. So, I'll borrow one of the horses and be out of your way."

Dumbstruck, they allowed Gindar to push past them. When he cleared the door, Hassan came to life and leapt after him. "Secure the rear gate. I'll stop him at the stable, if I can," he called to Aminah as he disappeared into the night.

She chased after Hassan, but then veered toward the gate. If Gindar managed to escape the stable, she wondered what hope she had of stopping him. Aminah checked to be sure the gate was bolted before melting into the shadows to wait. He would be forced to dismount to open it. Somehow she would delay him long enough for Hassan to catch up.

Barra's shrill scream sliced through the darkness, and Aminah ran for the stable. She found her standing just inside, a lighted lamp held high in her trembling hand. Aminah would have screamed, too, had not the scene sucked the air from her lungs. Hassan lay twisted beneath a stallion, its eyes wide and white. The horse twitched and danced, its hooves churning the dry earth around Hassan's motionless body.

SEVEN

BADR STARED INTO a polished silver mirror and brushed her long dark tresses. Aladdin paced the room behind her. He stopped and dropped his hands on her narrow shoulders. She shrugged them away.

"Whom would you rather rule in your father's stead?" he asked, the color rising in his cheeks. But the question was rhetorical for Aladdin. He knew Badr wanted Al-Kal'as for herself.

When she didn't answer, he tried again to touch her, but she lashed out with the mirror. He was quick enough to save his knuckles.

"Then take the city for yourself," he said in frustration. "If you think you can." No woman in their world had ever ruled in a man's stead, so strong were the traditions.

Badr slowly turned to face him. "There won't be a city to rule if you keep draining the coffers," she said icily. "What sense is there in your feeding the vermin in our streets? They are lazy and shiftless, and therefore they can serve us no good purpose. And they will die anyway when we become beggars ourselves."

"You are wrong, my Full Moon of Full Moons. Go to the far reaches of the city and see the work these people have done in return for a little sustenance. And see what has become of Beggars' Corridor."

Without a word, Badr went back to her brushing. Aladdin threw up his hands. "I have a few complaints of my own," he said. "I'll start with this Ashraf you dragged home. Why is he here? A pall covers the room whenever he enters—he is a dark presence."

"My personal seer," Badr answered. "I'm sending him away soon. Does that make you happy?"

"Will he travel with that man you released from the dungeons?"

She flinched, but quickly recovered. Still, Aladdin noticed.

"Oh, yes, I know about him. I even know his name— Rashid. I am not as thick in the head as you believe, my love. Rumor has it he's somehow linked to the beggar girl and the missing lamp. Would you like to tell me how he fits into the picture?"

The Princess laughed. "Figure it out for yourself, if you're so clever."

"Why must you brood over the lamp?" he asked. "And Aminah?"

"She spirited me to Makkah," Badr hissed.

"Yes, the cunning girl. But she is gone from here and will stay hidden, I'd wager. Free yourself from the lamp's curse, Badr," he pleaded.

"If you were a man of honor, you'd seek to avenge my shame," she said.

Aladdin sighed. "I am sorry, not for your shame but for your hard heart, Badr. The girl did not wrong you. You threw the lamp, intent on harming her. After that, Aminah was only protecting herself."

"Idiot!" she screamed. "Once the little slut discovered the lamp's power, she should have returned it. And you! Had you bothered to share the lamp's secret, this wouldn't have happened. Go away! The sight of you sickens me. Go! Mingle with your own kind. From the streets you came, Aladdin, and there you should have stayed."

He took a step back, as if he'd been struck, and they stood staring silently at each other. "You are fearless, I'll grant you that," he said at last. "Any other sultan would make quick work of the likes of you."

"Don't insult my father's name by calling yourself a sultan. And don't threaten me. You are toothless, Aladdin—dispatching me or anyone else, for that matter, is not in your blood. So stay out of my way, and I'll let you play at being sultan—for now."

"As you wish," Aladdin said coolly, and with a deep bow, he left her.

Trembling with rage, he leaned against the wall outside her door. He was as much angered with himself as with Badr. How had he been so blind as not to see past her façade? Was she so masterful at the art of deception? Yes, he realized, for she had masked her heart from him—that is, until she'd learned his true heritage. No matter how she might try, Badr seemed incapable of caring for a boy from the streets.

For a moment, Aladdin wished he still possessed the lamp and could wish himself a new existence. But then he smiled grimly, remembering the lamp had given him this one. *I'll stay for now,* he thought. *And I will help Aminah.*

WITH ALADDIN GONE, Badr moved into an adjoining room. "We're alone," she said.

Silken drapes along the wall swayed, and Saladin emerged from behind them. "Aladdin is a threat to our cause," observed the Captain of the Guard. "He knows too much."

"Yes," said the Princess. "He might even be foolish enough to cause trouble."

"Then he must be eliminated," said Saladin. "A sad accident, of course."

"No!" Badr turned away. "No," she repeated softly. "I will not kill him. I've made threats, I know, but . . . We'll keep close watch instead. If he becomes a stumbling block, we can restrain him."

Saladin stepped around to face her. "But . . . I thought you wished to be free of him."

She shrugged. "Perhaps." Then Badr stiffened, and her eyes narrowed. "Yes, I do. Two sultans cannot rule the same city. But nevertheless—"

A sudden commotion outside the apartment sent Saladin sliding back behind the draperies. Badr hurried to pull open the door and found her two eunuch guards barring Ashraf's way. One of the giants had the cleric by the throat. As she watched, the old man grasped the heavy arm that held him. The eunuch drew in a sharp breath at the cleric's touch and snatched back his hand as if he'd been burned.

"Stand aside," Ashraf ordered in his dry whisper.

The guards glanced at the Princess, who nodded, and with obvious relief, they allowed the cleric to pass. He strode by Badr as the door snapped shut behind them, and into the room where Saladin was hidden, calling out the Captain's name.

"How did you know I was here?" Saladin asked, pushing aside the layers of silk. He was unable to mask his irritation.

"Knowing is his business," said Badr, also sounding peevish. "Why are you here, cleric?"

"I bear grim tidings," Ashraf answered, and though his voice maintained its same, monotonous pitch, Badr could see he was distraught. There was an uncharacteristic twitch near his eyes, which darted nervously about the room. "The Coffer of Hadim Tebdil is missing."

Badr had seen the strange box only once—when Ashraf had packed it with his other possessions before they departed for Al-Kal'as. It wasn't until they were on the road that the cleric had revealed the coffer's essential part in his plan. Without it, his chances for success were greatly diminished.

Badr's hands knotted into tiny fists. "How could this happen?" she demanded through clenched teeth. Had she not seen the cleric's effect on her eunuch, the Princess might have attempted throttling Ashraf herself.

"I might ask you the same question," he replied.

At his impertinent tone, Badr's fingers flew to the dagger

concealed in her robe, but Saladin's touch cooled her temper. "Take care, cleric," he said. "Is not the box enchanted? Can you not sense magical things?"

Ashraf turned a disdainful eye on the Captain of the Guard. "The coffer is the antithesis of magic—its opposite, if you will. And so it cannot be sensed like a jinni's lamp or a flying carpet."

"How could this happen?" Badr cried again.

"Nothing seemed disturbed," Ashraf continued, without looking at the Princess, "and yet the coffer had been carefully removed. As the corridor always has a sentry, I must assume you have a thief among the Palace Guard."

When Saladin didn't respond, Badr turned a questioning eye to him and noticed the deep crease in his brow. "What is it?" she asked.

"One of my men has gone missing—two days now. Because the punishment for leaving one's post is . . . unpleasant, it happens rarely. This particular guard has been with me for some years, and I thought him steadfast. But now I suspect he will not return."

"No," Badr said in the quiet voice that Saladin had learned to fear. "He will not return because you will slit his throat and leave him for the jackals. Bring the box back to us, Saladin."

ALADDIN WAS ALONE. He'd sent away his advisers, even his Grand Vizier. Usually he enjoyed their company, but today their council had become a constant prattling that irritated him. He needed the quiet to think about Badr.

His first attempt at frustrating her quest to find Aminah had failed. Realizing Rashid must be key to her plans, Aladdin had thought to steal him away, to take him someplace far from Al-Kal'as. However, Rashid was nowhere to be found.

"Where is he hidden?" Aladdin said aloud to the empty room, though he'd already determined to abandon his search. He would shift his attention to Ashraf instead.

Aladdin wasn't foolish enough to defy the Princess openly. Normally, a woman wouldn't offer a threat, but he was an interloper in Badr's territory. As the only child of the Sultan, she had allies throughout the palace—allies who felt Aladdin had no right to his new position of power.

He was unsure whom among the old guard at the palace he could trust, but he'd brought in a few of his own people—old friends from his humble beginnings. He would use them to mount a secret mission to abduct Ashraf, though the task had suddenly become more daunting.

Aladdin had spies, too. He knew about the missing coffer—and the missing guardsman who was thought to have stolen it. Saladin and his men had scoured the palace and the city to unearth clues to his disappearance, but had found nothing. From the corridor outside Badr's apartment, Aladdin had heard her raging at the news. Since then, she guarded the cleric every second of the day.

Pacing his chambers, Aladdin grappled with the problem of separating Ashraf from the formidable force Badr had assigned to guard him. To do it without being detected seemed impossible.

A rap at the door interrupted his thoughts, and he looked up to see Idris, his new Royal Teller of Tales, stepping into the room. "How did you get past the sentries?" he asked angrily. "I told them I was not to be disturbed."

"And I told them you sent for me," said Idris. "I can be very convincing."

Something in Idris's manner kept Aladdin from summoning the guards to drag the storyteller away. Rather than insolence or threats, he sensed an ally. In fact, when he thought about it, he'd felt that in Idris from the first moment they'd met. Still, he was cautious.

"Whatever brings you had better be worth the risk you've just taken," said Aladdin.

"Like you, my whole life has been a risk," Idris answered with a smile. "Don't look surprised, my Sultan. I lived in the streets, so the tale of your origins is known to me. We are brothers under the skin."

Aladdin laughed. "I suspected as much," he said. "Tell me, Idris, why have you come?"

"The truth?"

"Of course."

"I am Aminah's friend," Idris said.

Aladdin could only stare.

"I was the one who used the lamp to send Badr away. Otherwise, she would have killed us. Or rather, Saladin would have. I'm sorry, but there was little other choice."

"How is it Badr doesn't recognize you?" Aladdin asked. "And why have you returned?"

"When the Princess finally found us, I stayed out of sight. After I sent her away, I left the lamp with Aminah and headed to Makkah."

"You followed Badr?"

"No. I wanted to make the pilgrimage, but I did stumble upon her. And she had that wretched Ashraf with her. I admit

I spied on the Princess—I had to know why she'd secured the cleric's services. He makes a life of finding and destroying demons, like your former jinni. She will use him to locate Aminah and the lamp, and when he does, my friend is dead."

"Why are you telling me this? How do you know I'm not in league with my wife? Then your life and Aminah's would be forfeit."

Again, Idris smiled. "One who feeds the poor of Al-Kal'as will not be in league with the likes of the Full Moon of Full Moons. Pardon me for saying so, but I find your match with her unimaginable."

Aladdin's throat closed as he thought of Badr. None was outwardly more beautiful, and she had led him to believe another sort of loveliness lay within her. But then he realized the deception was not all hers—beauty and the promise of power had intoxicated and deluded him. "I did not use the lamp wisely," he finally managed to say.

"But you are acting wisely now. Did you know Aminah uses the lamp to bless the lives of others? Every full moon she finds someone with a heart like yours—someone who will use the jinni's gifts to help a host of others. Aladdin, you have become the very sort of person she would choose."

Again unable to speak, Aladdin nodded, acknowledging the kindness in Idris's words.

"I must save Aminah and the lamp from Badr," Idris continued. "That's why I am here now, and why I must leave."

"Leave? How will leaving help?"

"As you know, Saladin is gone from Al-Kal'as to look for Ashraf's stolen coffer."

"Yes, though I don't understand why this box is so important."

"How long he and the cleric will search, I'm unsure," said Idris. "Eventually, they plan to follow Rashid's lead in their quest to find Aminah. Did you know Rashid was the one who gave her up to Badr in the first place? And now he has convinced Saladin he can find her."

"Is he right?"

"I doubt it, but I won't take the smallest chance. By going to Aminah now, I can arrange it so Ashraf will be unable to sense the lamp."

"How will you 'arrange' this?" asked Aladdin. "And where is Aminah? No, don't tell me. If I don't know, my tongue can't slip. But I still don't understand why you came to me."

"I'm asking you to provide me with an excuse for being away. I'd leave Al-Kal'as and not return, but my sudden disappearance would arouse Badr's suspicions," said Idris. "Besides, I need to be here for other reasons—matters best left secret, I assure you. So, could you say that I received news my mother is dying and that you have allowed me to be at her deathbed? I will take care of Aminah and return with no one the wiser."

"Hiding Aminah won't stop their search," said Aladdin, "but I can keep you abreast of Badr's plans. What shall I say is your destination?"

"Damascus. It was my home."

Aladdin gripped Idris's hand. "You may have wondered if I wish to possess the lamp again. I admit I've dreamed of its return to me. Are you certain I can be trusted?"

"Yes," said Idris.

Aladdin nodded. "Indeed, you needn't worry. I'm pleased you came to me; I was at wit's end trying to find a way to help your friend. Now, what do you need for the trip?" He took up a small, portable writing desk and scribbled a note.

"This is leave to take whatever you need for the journey," he explained. "And may Allah bless your every step. While you're away, I'll do my best to make Badr believe I've lost interest in her pursuit of the lamp. That way it will be easier for me to watch her, and who knows what I might discover to help our cause?"

Idris extended a grateful hand to take the note. "I want you to know about Ashraf's coffer," he said. "He calls it the Coffer of Hadim Tebdil."

Aladdin looked puzzled. "The Coffer of Impotent Transformations? What does it mean?"

"I think I know. And I think it could be the solution we are seeking."

"But the coffer has been stolen."

"Yes. However, I believe I know where to find it," said Idris.

eight

As Barra moved the frightened horse away from Hassan, Aminah fell to her knees beside his broken body. She sobbed in relief at the rise and fall of his chest, for he'd seemed lifeless at first glance. Hassan's right leg was bent at an unnatural angle, and Aminah could see it was shattered. His right arm had fared no better.

Gindar—or was it Omar?—was huddled in the far corner of the stable. Blood trickled from a gash on his forehead, and his eyes were glazed. Aminah knew demons were impervious to harm, and so Jinni must be right—he had become human.

Barra returned to kneel by Aminah. "In their tussle, Hassan fell beneath the stallion," she whispered. "The noise and tumult spooked the beast. If Omar hadn't come to his senses and pulled him away . . ."

"What shall we do, Barra? Dare we move him?"

"Stay here," Barra answered. "I'll go for a physician."

"Wait! Should we bind Omar . . . Gindar?" Aminah asked.

"The stallion's hoof drove Gindar from his head. Without the glitter of gold, you're likely safe."

Omar blinked against the lantern's light. Though only semiconscious, he seemed to know Aminah was near. "Forgive me," he murmured.

THOUGH SERIOUS, the breaks in Hassan's arm and leg were not as crippling as Aminah had feared. The physician Barra had dragged from his bed had set the limbs in the stable.

"He is fortunate this wasn't worse. A hoof might have crushed his skull. And yours, too," he said, turning to Omar.

"However, Hassan's breaks are severe enough," the physician continued, glancing at his unconscious patient. "He will be three or four months healing, and he still may walk with a limp for some time after that."

Later, as the sun rose, Hassan awakened in his quarters, squirming in agony. Aminah coaxed the mixture left by the physician down his throat, and before long, the foul-tasting liquid had controlled the worst of the pain. When he was finally comfortable and slumber beckoned, Aminah called in Barra and Omar. Omar rushed to Hassan's bedside and dropped to his knees. "I shall never, never forgive myself for this!" he cried.

Aminah was amazed by the human quality in Omar's reaction, but Hassan simply waved a hand, as if to dismiss the blame. "From what I understand, I'd be dead if you hadn't pulled me free," he whispered, his voice groggy. "No, Omar, I don't fault you. Gindar, perhaps, but not you."

Omar bowed his head. "I do not make a very good human. Yes, the demon inside has been shackled, and it is quite humbling. I have a terrible headache besides. At least I am now aware of Gindar's presence, and being aware, I believe I can keep him at bay."

"That's good news," said Hassan.

"Yes," Aminah agreed, taking the hand of his uninjured arm. "Which means I must go on without you."

Hassan pulled away from her and tried to sit up. He groaned and fell back, breathing heavily. "You . . . are . . . not leaving," he gasped.

"I did my best to dissuade—" Barra began, but Aminah's fierce glare silenced her.

"Do not go, I beg you," Hassan whispered.

"I don't want to leave you," she said, her eyes welling with tears. "But too much is at stake to wait for you to heal. What will happen to us without the lamp?"

"We could live like everyone else. We don't need the lamp to be happy."

"Ella will die," she murmured. "I can't allow that to happen, dear one. Please understand."

"Will Omar travel with you? No! It matters not. You mustn't go, Aminah!"

"If I go, I'll need him. Besides, it wouldn't be wise to travel alone." She leaned in and kissed his forehead. "We'll talk about this later, after you sleep again."

Hassan struggled to stay awake as the effects of the physician's concoction took full effect. "Yes, we'll talk later," he murmured, his eyes already closed. Aminah kissed him again, her tears staining both her face and his.

She stepped away, and then wept bitterly at the sure knowledge that she would leave Hassan behind to chase the lamp. There was some comfort in knowing Barra would care for him as if he were her own son, but still, she marveled that she could abandon him like this.

Aminah returned to Hassan's side, kissing him over and over. But at the same time, she felt an uncompromising sense of urgency pulling her away. Like a cancer, the emptiness left by her departed magic threatened to consume her. Again she stepped away from Hassan, throwing off her robe to reveal the traveling garb beneath.

"You won't reconsider?" asked Barra.

Aminah bowed her head, trying to take control of her emotions. "Yes," she answered at last. "I will reconsider with every step I take, but there is a force within I can't fight. Hassan was right; magic has a way of causing trouble."

Barra hugged her and then kissed each cheek. "May Allah protect and guide you. And as for you," she said to Omar, "behave yourself or you'll answer to me." She kissed him as well, then stoically returned to sit with Hassan.

Aminah had steeled herself for this moment, but still she couldn't make herself move. Omar tugged at her robe, and at last, without looking back, she allowed him to lead her from the room.

"I fear being with you should Gindar surface," she said, brushing at her cheeks as they made their way to the stable. "Will you guarantee I'll see nothing of him?"

"I hate him more than you do," said Omar. "I will try my best to smother the creature."

The horses were packed and waiting in the stable. They led them through the rear gate, locking it behind them. Aminah stared at Omar, searching his eyes one last time for Gindar. She sighed nervously, and then mounted her stallion.

"We must hurry," said Omar, trotting ahead. "We cannot chance missing the caravan in Damascus."

No caravans were scheduled to depart from Tyre toward Al-Kal'as for weeks, but they left more frequently from the larger city to the east. To travel great distances through treacherous country without the protection of a caravan was suicide, so they expected to find Idris waiting to join one.

When they arrived in Damascus, they discovered a caravan was leaving the next day, but there was no sign of Idris. They stayed out of sight, hoping to catch him unawares, but when the cavalcade formed, he still hadn't appeared. Having no other reasonable option, Aminah and Omar took their places in the train and left the city.

"What other route could he have taken?" Aminah asked.

"Perhaps he went on to Baghdad," said Omar, "which means we will find him waiting there for our caravan."

But when their procession marched away from Baghdad two weeks later, it was without Idris.

ANOTHER TWO WEEKS after leaving Baghdad and crossing a rugged range of mountains, the caravan arrived in Hamadhan. During another month on the trail, their southerly route dropped to the desert then back up into the mountains until they reached the city of Shiraz. For Aminah, their slow progress intensified her anxiety over not knowing what had become of Idris and the lamp. And over her ever-increasing separation from Hassan.

The terrain was no less gentle as they traveled eastward from Shiraz, but after another agonizing three weeks, the caravan descended into the Great Desert. Being in the desert rather than the mountains meant less chance of bandits, and everyone breathed more easily. They stayed the night at an oasis near the base of the foothills, and a caravan traveling toward Baghdad shared their campsite.

Cool breezes wafting downward from the mountain slopes stirred the palm fronds—and the aquatic grasses sprouting in the pools of the oasis. The soft noises of caravans at rest floated toward Aminah from all directions: the whuffling and snorting of camels and horses, a wife calling plaintively to her husband, the crackling of cooking fires. *Such a pleasant spot,* she thought as she gazed on the moonlit water. But the rippling reflection in the pool reminded her of the sea—of gazing down on the silver waves while resting her head against Hassan's shoulder. With a sob, she looked away, following the light's shimmering path back to its source.

Her misery only doubled when she saw that the moon was swelling toward fullness. The days preceding a full moon were usually filled with excitement—with possibilities—but there would be no wishes this time. *Oh, Idris, where are you?* she pleaded silently. *Rather than making a marriage, you've prevented one.*

Voices reached from across the pool, and soon two women

bearing leather water jars appeared nearby. Not feeling up to exchanging pleasantries, Aminah started back to Omar, who was preparing their evening meal.

As she passed through the palm grove, a face peered from behind a tree trunk, and her heart stopped. The man's eyes caught the moonlight as he turned and disappeared into the night. Aminah thought she recognized him, and for a terrible moment, she thought she might faint. But her head cleared, and she crept after the dark figure.

Staying out of sight, she watched him leave the palms and approach a campfire. Two other men sat near the flames, their features obscured. But when their friend approached, they stood and turned, the fire illuminating their faces. Aminah stifled an involuntary cry and fell to her knees. Shivering uncontrollably, she crawled away from the firelight until the darkness blanketed her. Then she stood and stumbled toward her campsite.

Soon Aminah heard Omar singing to himself—a song filled with odd-sounding words like *crackerjacks* and *threestrikes*—but the moment she burst from the trees, his lyrics trailed away.

"Aminah!" He left off stirring a pot and reached for the scimitar he'd picked up in Baghdad. "You look as though you have faced down Azráeel himself."

"Rashid," she whispered, cowering at the sounds slipping from her own lips. "And Saladin. They're here!"

"Rashid? And the Captain of the Guard? But how did they find us? How could they have known?"

But Aminah wasn't listening. Her eyes bored into the depths

of the palm grove. Suddenly she scurried outside the ring of firelight. "They mustn't see me," she whispered. "They're traveling in the other caravan, and I doubt it's an accident they're heading the way we came. And another man accompanies them. He is old and wizened, yet I feared him instantly. Do you think this is what led Idris to take . . ." Aminah paused, looking over her shoulder. "To take *it*? That he knew *they* were coming?"

"Hello there, Omar!" The voice startled them, and Aminah fled into the trees. "We are camped at the south end of the pool. Meet us there—say in an hour?" The man stepped from the darkness. "We're anxious to see if you are as good with the dice as you say."

"Yes, yes," said Omar, returning to his pot, his voice gruff and impatient.

Aminah rushed back to the fire and grabbed Omar's sleeve as the man went his way. "You're going off to play at games of chance? You'd break your oath not to tempt Gindar? I forbid you to leave my side tonight! That you'd even entertain such an idea—especially knowing Rashid and Saladin may strike at any moment."

"Of course I will not leave you," said Omar, shamefaced. "And just so you know, I have detected not a hint of Gindar since leaving home."

"Nevertheless, stay away from the dice. You must fight him in every way. I can't afford to lose you. Oh, if only you hadn't mislaid your magic, none of this would be happening!"

"Mislaid! Are you blaming me for losing my powers?" Even though it was Omar speaking, the voice was frigid—and an octave away from outrage.

"No, no. I didn't mean it that way," she said, pulling him away from the light. "It's just that without your magic at my fingertips, I feel all jumbled up inside—like a drunkard who doesn't know where to find his next mouthful of wine." Shivering, Aminah hugged herself. What hope did she have if she couldn't rely on Omar?

"I think we should leave," he said. "Strike out on our own, now that we have the desert ahead of us."

"But where would we go?" she asked.

"Ahead," Omar repeated. "Perhaps we can meet up with our caravan farther along the trail. If we cover our tracks, Saladin may believe we have turned back to warn Hassan."

"Ah, but you underestimate me."

Saladin stepped from the trees and in two long strides reached Aminah. She recognized the dagger he held to her neck by its ornate pommel. Shortly before Idris had spirited Badr and her guards to Makkah, Saladin had threatened to slit Barra's throat with its blade.

nine

AMINAH STOOD, rooted in place. Then fury and fear set her in motion. Ignoring Saladin's knife, she twisted away from him. But with unexpected speed and perfect timing, the old man she had noticed earlier arrived at Saladin's side, blocking her path. Rashid stood behind, keeping Omar at bay with a scimitar.

She bounced off the old one's decaying body and turned to run the other way. But like a striking cobra, Saladin's hand shot forward to snare her.

Again, Aminah felt his dagger at her throat. "I was sorely disappointed when I missed the last opportunity to spill your blood," he said. "Now I plan to spill but a little at a time— until you give me the lamp. Then who knows—I might spare you long enough for you to have the honor of once again see-ing the Princess's face."

The old man fell back to stand by Rashid, whispering in his ear.

"Ashraf says the lamp is not here," Rashid said to Saladin. "Our journey is not ended."

Aminah locked eyes with Rashid. "You sniveling jackal," she said. "I'd hoped Badr had done me one favor, but here you are, still alive."

He thrust the scimitar into Ashraf's grasp and stepped closer. His nose was almost touching Aminah's when he answered, his fetid breath choking her. "I will enjoy watching you bleed."

"So, cleric," said Saladin, "I thought you were unable to sense the lamp, as things stand. How do you know, then, that it is not in the girl's pack?"

"It is common sense that tells me," said Ashraf. Aminah strained to hear words no louder than the stirring of dried leaves. "She would have attempted to use the lamp to escape, once she'd laid eyes on you. But we have been watching, and I did not see her produce it, did you? I tell you, the one who has the coffer has the lamp—although I had hoped finding the girl would mean finding the box as well. Saladin, if Aminah had had the lamp without the coffer, I would have sensed its magic. But go ahead, search her belongings if you wish."

"Despite what you say, cleric, I believe I will," said Saladin. Ashraf grunted in disgust as Saladin's hands combed over Aminah's body. Meanwhile, Rashid tore through her pack and Omar's.

"You've filled out nicely, for a beggar girl," said Saladin with a cruel smile.

Aminah cringed under his assault but didn't bother with a useless struggle to escape. Rather, she blocked out Saladin's probing fingers and thought of Hassan's gentle caress. Soon the man lost interest when it was plain she hadn't hidden the lamp in the folds of her robe.

"Nothing," Rashid called to his companions.

"Then we step into the desert, my dear," Saladin said. "You and I and my dagger shall have a most cordial conversation." His pleasant, unhurried tone chilled Aminah's heart.

Omar jumped forward, but Ashraf smashed the flat of the scimitar against the side of his head with such force that the sound echoed from the trees. He crumpled to the ground as Aminah cried out. Rashid laughed and started to follow Saladin, but the Captain of the Guard motioned him to stay. His disappointment was palpable.

Saladin pushed her in front of him, and Aminah stumbled. As she pitched forward, death whispered a hand's-breadth above her head. It was followed by a dull thud, the sound of a knife plunging up to its hilt into a melon.

Aminah rolled aside, looking back. Saladin had sunk to his knees. He seemed puzzled as his gaze wandered down to the arrow protruding from his chest. Aminah could see that he thought to raise his hand to pluck it out. But then life fled his features, and he toppled forward.

Rashid screamed and ran toward the watering hole, but Ashraf collared him. Staying flat on the ground, Aminah watched the cleric steer Rashid into the desert at a right angle to the arrow's course.

Shouting filled the air, followed by more screaming. Though it was difficult to think straight, Aminah decided to follow Ashraf's lead. She crawled over to Omar just as he began to stir and guided him on hands and knees away from the firelight and into the desert.

Once under cover of darkness, she thought to stand, but as she rose, Omar pulled her down again. "Bandits," he whispered. "We must distance ourselves from the caravan. Keep low."

Standing but hunched over, they scuttled deeper into the desert, and though Aminah thought they traced Ashraf's path, there was no sign of him or Rashid.

"Over there," said Omar, pointing toward a rock outcropping clearly visible under the gibbous moon.

"I thought there was strength in numbers," Aminah whispered. "Two caravans together should have discouraged bandits."

"That is true, for a regular band of scruffy ruffians, but this is an army of thieves—hundreds of them. They are well trained, from the look of things, and ruthless. Few in either train will live through the night."

As if to confirm Omar's chilling prediction, a fresh chorus of shouting and screaming reached their ears. "Quick, we must make the rocks," he urged.

Standing straight, they sprinted for the outcropping. But as Aminah was about throw herself onto the stone face and climb to safety, she heard the dull thud of hooves. The desert sands had deadened their sound, but as the clutch of bandits veered toward them, the horses were soon clip-clopping across rockier ground.

"Do something!" Aminah cried, tugging on the sleeve of Omar's robe.

"As you wish!" He snapped his fingers, and then stared at his hand in momentary disbelief.

Aminah looked on in dismay. Panicked, she had forgotten Jinni was powerless—and so had he.

"What did you expect?" demanded Omar, misreading Aminah's expression as anger. "Do not blame me! This is your fault for losing the lamp."

"My fault! You should have sensed someone was tampering with it. Instead, you were too busy . . ." Her voice trailed away. The bandits, still astride their mounts, had encircled them.

Headgear garbed the bandits' faces, leaving only slits for eyes that gleamed in the cool moonlight. Sharp smells of unwashed bodies—both horses and men—mingled with the leathery odor of saddles, and in the pungent silence surrounding them, Aminah could hear anguished wailing from the distant oasis.

At last, one of the bandits spoke. Even in the dark, Aminah could see that his attire was far richer than that of his comrades, and as he urged his mount forward a few steps, she could tell he was cleaner, too.

"Search them," he said.

It took the filthy hands only moments to find their money belts, which, when emptied, produced a chorus of cheers.

"Shall I slit their throats?" asked one of the men.

"The girl interests me. Kill the other."

"No!" cried Aminah.

"Ah, you care for him," said the well-dressed bandit, his smile alluringly gentle. "A brother? Or a lover? It matters not, as I have use for neither. But you, my dear, are another story. We need a cook—ours recently died from eating his own swill." The circle of thieves laughed at their master's wit.

"As luck would have it, Omar is the best cook I know,"

said Aminah in a voice far bolder than she felt. Indeed, Omar had begun to outshine Barra in the kitchen. "I beg you, give him a try."

The man reached up and loosened the cloth that covered his features. Aminah saw the striking face of a man in his middle years. "Your brother is a cook? Or is he your lover? We did not establish this fact."

"Omar is my uncle," Aminah replied.

The bandit's eyes held hers. Though they danced with laughter, she could see the hard glint of cruelty beneath the surface, and her stomach clenched in fear. "He prepares meals fit for a sultan," she said, her voice faltering. "I—I promise you won't be sorry to let him live."

The thief smiled again, and it was so disarming that Aminah almost lowered her guard. *Like the serpent that beguiled Eve,* she thought.

"I am Hammarab," the man said, with a slight nod of his head. "Commander of this rather dubious army. And you?"

"Aminah."

"Well, Aminah, I will grant your Uncle Omar a turn in my kitchen. My men were too quick with scimitar and bow, disposing of my choices at the oasis. I only pray you are right about him."

"Then your prayers shall be answered," she replied.

"Ah, the wit! The boldness! This is no ordinary girl, my friends," he said to his fellows. "She may be the greatest of the spoils." Hammarab climbed from his mount and unfastened a rug strapped behind the saddle. "Ahmad," he said to the nearest thief, "take two others and inspect the oasis. Lead the wagons to this spot."

As Ahmad and the others galloped away, Hammarab approached Aminah, kicking aside the rocks and clearing a place on the hard ground. Unrolling the carpet, the thief lord motioned for her to sit. She almost refused but then thought better of it.

To her surprise, Hammarab sat down beside her. She looked toward Omar, but the other men had surrounded him. They swept him away, all the while quizzing him enthusiastically on whether or not he could prepare one dish or the other.

"An army—even an army of thieves—puts its belly above all concerns," Hammarab said.

"Even above the fear of death?" Aminah dared ask.

He laughed at her biting tone. "Perhaps not at the precise moment death looks one in the eye, but if a warrior survives death's gaze, it is food that brings him solace. Or perhaps a woman." He reached forward to brush aside a stray lock of Aminah's hair. She flinched at the movement, and he laughed again, amused by the dread clawing its way across her face.

Aminah stared at the ground, waiting for her heart's rapid drumbeat to slow. Finally she managed to say, "Your men may look forward to the finest of solace. Uncle Omar's fare will provide more comfort than a sultan's harem." Then, to disguise the tremor that threatened her voice, she rose and called toward the knot of thieves surrounding Omar. "Uncle Omar! You are to be Lord Hammarab's chef. Come! Let him choose the first meal for you to prepare."

"Not now," Hammarab said softly. "The man is occupied."

The thieves had kindled a small fire on a ledge of rock with faggots and dried dung. She wondered why they bothered—surely this wasn't to be their campsite.

"To illuminate their game," said Hammarab, as if reading her thoughts.

At that moment, one of the bandits reached inside his robe. In a space before the fire, he rolled the dice. Aminah watched with alarm as Omar's shoulders tightened and his back grew rigid. Gindar couldn't resist a game of chance.

A wave of hopelessness engulfed her. She was alone now. Because Gindar would remain surrounded by thieves and gamblers, Omar might never resurface. Aminah swallowed back the sob that rose in her throat, but then cried out as a piercing shriek cut through the night. It was a death cry, carried from the oasis on a gust of desert wind.

"Don't be frightened," said Hammarab, his hand lighting on her shoulder. Whimpering, she slid away from his touch and moved to the edge of the rug, wishing desperately to be home and in Hassan's tight embrace.

"I understand how you must feel," said Hammarab, following her gaze across the silvery sands. "No, that's not so. I can only guess."

"And why should a man such as you bother to speculate?" she asked in a whisper.

He turned his eyes on her without answering. The silence stretched between them, but Aminah dared not break it. Suddenly Hammarab slapped his thigh and said, "Come, let's talk of other things. You must wonder how I ended up like this, yes? A product of the streets, I'm afraid—abandoned there as a five-year-old."

"And you learned to survive by your wits and your fast fingers," said Aminah.

"This is something you understand," he said. "I can hear it in your voice. How is that?"

Hammarab waited in silence as Aminah struggled with her misgivings about answering. She wondered how much to tell a man who cared so little for a human life, but finally she could see no harm in telling the truth. "I, too, was left alone in the streets, though I was twelve. My parents died."

"I knew it!" he said, his eyes lighting. "I sensed we had something in common."

A cheer rose from the knot of gamblers. Gindar stood, shaking his fists heavenward in triumph. Though disgusted by the sight, Aminah realized with a jolt that everything she hated about him was of little consequence when compared to Hammarab's brutality. Gindar's existence wasn't soaked in the blood of countless others. Glancing at the thief lord, she vowed to escape no matter the cost.

"A chance to regain our losses," said one of the thieves, in a voice that made it clear Gindar had no choice in the matter. He plunked down his winnings and shoveled up the dice, but the creaking of wooden wheels stopped the game.

Hammarab stood as the wagons drew near. "You'll have to wait for your revenge," he said to the gamers, who grumbled but didn't argue. He offered a hand to help Aminah up. She stood on her own, and his eyes narrowed.

"Ride in the first wagon, along with your uncle," he said, brusquely. "We'll talk again at the Citadel."

Before Aminah could ask about the Citadel, Hammarab was

astride his mount and, along with his band of riders, racing toward the oasis. Gindar joined her to watch them go.

"A decent lot," he said. "Gave me a chance to win back our gold."

Crestfallen, Aminah didn't answer. It was as if she'd once again been forsaken in the alleys of Al-Kal'as.

◑

THE WAGONS RATTLED UPWARD into the hill country. With harder ground beneath the wheels, they rolled through the night with increased speed.

Aminah was uncomfortable riding amid the plunder piled high in the wagon bed. At first she moved away from a jewel box, imagining bandits prying it from the cold fingers of a corpse. But the booty was everywhere, and she couldn't escape the terrible images in her head. Eventually, numbed by the horror, she fell asleep on a mound of silk pillows.

At last, the procession stopped, and Aminah awoke. The moon was waning, and the sky, hinting at dawn, silhouetted ragged mountaintops. She pulled her eyes from the snow-capped peaks and glanced at Gindar. He was rutting through the booty like a pig through its slops, and she wondered, a deep ache in her chest, if she'd indeed lost Omar forever.

Aminah sat up to find the wagons stopped at the edge of a clear pool, nestled in a small valley. A few trees graced the banks, and it seemed to her a pleasant spot to rest. Needing to distance herself from Gindar, she was about to crawl down and stretch her legs when the driver stood, raising his arms.

"Sea of Darkness, in the name of Julnar receive us!" he called over the dark water. In the next instant, he took the reins and urged the horses into the pool.

It seemed an odd way to water the animals, but Aminah wasn't concerned until the pond began pouring over the sides of the wagon. Confused, she scrambled to get out, but Gindar grabbed her from behind, pinning her arms. She held her breath and struggled against him as the wagon slipped beneath the calm, black surface.

Aminah's instincts demanded she push upward, but she couldn't break Gindar's hold. Depleted air erupted from her tortured lungs.

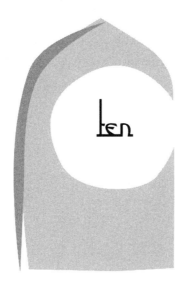

ten

SUCCULENT AIR, sweet as honey, whistled through her teeth. Stunned, Aminah swept an arm through the dry atmosphere in front of her dripping face. Then, as if by some enchantment, her clothing and hair were instantly dry.

As the panic receded, her breathing slowed, and she peered about in silent wonder. Deep into earth, water suspended overhead like the inside of a dark blue bowl, the wagons rolled along a stone roadway. Soon they passed through a tall, arched door hewn in a wall of solid rock and into the torchlight of an underground hideaway.

A great cavern greeted them, large enough to stable a hundred horses and more. There were also stonework pens filled with livestock, and a cacophony of clucking, braying, and bleating greeted the wagons. Yet, with all the animals, plus the hundreds of torches lighting the place, the air was not foul, and Aminah soon noticed that a steady breeze coursed continuously through the great hall, up a wide staircase carved from the living rock, and down the many corridors that branched off in various directions.

The wagon train passed the stables and animal pens and started down a wide avenue. "We're heading to the storehouse," said Gindar, weighing a gold trinket in his hand. "I hope they show us at least one of the treasure rooms."

Aminah rounded on him angrily. "You knew!"

Gindar grinned. "My gambling cronies told me of the pool. We thought we'd have a bit of fun at your expense."

"What? You're a bandit now?" Aminah turned away. "Just looking at you makes me ill."

Gindar's arms encircled her. "Now, now. Don't pretend to hate me. I'm more of a man than your baker, you know."

With a shriek, Aminah wrenched free of his embrace. Spinning about, she flailed at him. He was chuckling when her fist dug into his eye. He screeched and toppled over.

Their guards roared with laughter, and Aminah rounded on them with unbridled fury. They only laughed harder, shoving her onto the silk pillows. She lay there, eyes stinging, until someone touched her shoulder.

Aminah wheeled about to knock the hand away, but it was Omar's stricken face that greeted her. "Aminah," he whispered. "Have I done it again? Have I allowed Gindar to take me?"

She flung her arms about his neck. "Yes, but you've come back to me," she murmured in his ear. "Stay away from the dice, Uncle Omar, and the treasure rooms. They are more than Gindar can resist. You must fight him harder than ever. You must!"

"It is more difficult than I believed," he said mournfully. "But I will do my best. I do not relish another punch in the eye to bring me to my senses."

"Come on, you two," ordered one of the guards. "You can help us unload."

They climbed down but stood to the side while thieves, like ants on a sweetmeat, swarmed the wagon. Alone for a moment, Aminah and Omar stood, surveying the cavern.

"Escape is unlikely," Omar said. "We are buried under a mountain, and who can guess whether or not the waters would part for us?"

"He called this place the Citadel," said Aminah. "It's certainly not what I expected. Still, it is well named."

"You there! Omar, is it?"

They turned to find an enormous bandit leaning on a walking stick. The man made two of Omar, and his greasy, black beard could have hidden Aminah altogether. They couldn't help but stare, and not only at his tremendous bulk. Their eyes settled on his left knee—which, along with everything below it, was missing. A stout silver rod extended to the ground from just above where his kneecap should have been. A serpent wrought of gold curled about the rod from top to bottom, and torchlight winked from rubies and emeralds encrusting its surface.

"Chewed off by a shark," said the giant. "After that, I mostly traded the life of a sea pirate for that of a land pirate, though with this"—he tapped the rod's iron tip on the stone roadway—"I don't see much action. Lost my leg savin' Hammarab's skin, so he give me this shiny peg and put me in charge of the day-to-day affairs of the Citadel. And the affair I'm about now is fetchin' our new cook. Now then, are you the fellow I'm after?"

Omar nodded.

"Follow me, and I'll introduce you to the jackal droppings that'll be your kitchen help. For your sake, the rumors better be true. Hammarab is expectin' a culinary master. I may seem the friendly sort at first sight, but don't be fooled. Spoil our dinner, and I'll plant the mark of my little snake here deep into your flabby buttocks." He gave the rod with its golden serpent a threatening shake. "By the by, I answer to the name of Iron Toe." For emphasis, he again tapped the silver shaft's iron tip against the stones.

"You'll find no cause to kick my uncle about," said Aminah. "There isn't a finer hand in the kitchen than Omar."

"Ah," said Iron Toe, seeming to take notice of her for the first time. "And you would be Hammarab's . . . new friend. I'm to fetch you as well. He has just returned with the animals from the caravan and awaits you."

He stood aside and ushered them past. They started back the way the wagons had come, marching in time to the *click-click* of the giant's iron-tipped peg.

When they neared the great stone staircase, Aminah saw Hammarab waiting at the top. Iron Toe stumped up the steps as she and Omar trailed behind. Giant and thief lord embraced, and then turned to examine their captives.

"I trust your passage to our Citadel was pleasant enough," said Hammarab.

"The entering caused me some discomfort," Aminah replied.

Hammarab grinned. "Yes, my men enjoy frightening our guests. But you must admit, the way in is quite spectacular."

"How did you find this place?" she asked, escape in mind. "And unlock its secrets?"

His grin widened, which proved to be his only answer. "Iron Toe," he said, "what do you think of our new cook?"

"If the girl is to be believed, we shall eat like the kings. If not, I'll be roastin' him for dinner myself." Iron Toe gave Omar's shoulder a companionable slap. "So come along, it is time to prove yourself."

Prodding Omar in the back with a sausagelike finger, Iron Toe steered him down a corridor leading to the scullery. As Aminah watched them disappear around a corner, the thought of being alone with Hammarab paralyzed her. She could still hear Iron Toe's tapping and held on to the sound like a lifeline. But soon it faded, and she was cut adrift.

Aminah's eyes remained locked on the spot where she'd last seen Omar, and Hammarab looked on in silence. Finally, he placed a hand on her arm, and she shivered.

"Why do you still fear me?" he asked.

Aminah lowered her eyes and shrugged.

Hammarab sighed. "Allow me to show you to your quarters," he said, his voice stiff, and still holding her arm, he guided her down another well-lit corridor. Her only thought was that he was leading her farther away from Omar.

THE CITADEL WAS A THIEVES' DEN, and yet the several rooms of Aminah's apartment might have been in a sultan's palace. Hammarab ushered her into the place and then, to her surprise and relief, excused himself, urging her to rest. "I have business that beckons," he said. "I will look in on you soon."

Aminah hoped "soon" meant several hours, or perhaps the next day—time enough for her to find a way out. As long as she was working her way toward Idris and the lamp, she could stave off the crippling anxiety brought on by the loss of her magic. But now that Hammarab had stopped her progress, panic gnawed at the gates of her mind, threatening a breach. Her fear of the thief lord only made things worse, and so to keep her wits about her, Aminah concentrated on trying to escape the Citadel. The fresh air flowing through the cavern entered from somewhere, she reasoned, and that somewhere might offer a path to freedom.

Aminah waited until Hammarab was well away before she tried the door, but it was barred against her leaving. How had she missed the sound of the bolt sliding into place? Despair overwhelmed her, and the gates in her head came crashing down. In a frantic, mindless rage, Aminah threw herself against the heavy bronze door, beating at it until her fists ran red.

At last, she stumbled back and dropped to one of the several diwans, so spent she hadn't the energy for tears. Sleep took her against her will, and she slumbered until a knock roused her. The bolt slid back, and a boy entered, balancing a silver tray.

"Omar sends greetings," the boy said, staggering under the weight of his burden. Omar had sent enough food for an army.

When Aminah sat up, the young servant gasped, his eyes moving from her hands to the diwan and back again. "What have you done to yourself, Miss?"

She came fully awake, aware now of the throbbing in her

fists. Blood stained her robe and patches of crimson dotted the diwan. "It's nothing," she answered shakily. "Leave the tray and go." Rooted in place, the boy continued to stare. "Please go," she said again, and he backed from the room.

Aminah ranged through the apartment until she found a washbasin. She cleaned away the desert dirt and the blood. Then she bound her hands with strips ripped from a muslin chemise she located in a chest. In other trunks she found clean clothing that, strange as it seemed, were women's garments close to her size. Aminah garbed herself in a fresh silk sarwal that was stylishly wide at the hips and narrow at the ankles, as well as a Dabiqi shirt and a rose colored robe.

She returned to the tray and forced herself to eat. Her meal had the unmistakable hallmarks of Omar's cooking. She shuffled the dishes, hoping to find a note, but was disappointed. Nevertheless, picking through the familiar morsels offered a little unexpected comfort.

When she finished, Aminah decided to examine the apartment in hopes of finding another way into the corridor. As she moved through the rooms, she came to a wall of mirrors and was confronted by her reflection wrapped in the new red robe. Though the workmanship was inferior, the robe still had the look of her enchanted thawb, and the sudden memory of it fanned the embers of her distress. *With Jinni's power, I'd be standing in Al-Kal'as instead of this dungeon,* she raged to herself. *I would have saved the lives lost at the oasis. I would have the lamp in my hands again.* That she had wished for lost magic to restore the very same lost magic didn't occur to her as senseless. The new storm brewing inside had clouded her thinking.

Aminah turned from the mirrors, driven by a surge of

panic, and rushed back to the bronze door, throwing herself against it with renewed fury. Then she wrenched at the ornate handle with such force that it seemed to come loose in her hand, tossing her to the floor. But the handle had only slipped from her fingers, her momentum sending her flying as the door moved inward. The boy had forgotten to bolt it!

Though stunned, Aminah managed a smile. Bloodying her hands hadn't been in vain after all; it had served to distract the child.

She eased the door closed and returned to the clothing chests. Rummaging through them, she found a heavy, woolen taylasan. She could bury herself deep inside the robe's hood, though that might draw as much attention as showing her face. Still, it seemed the better choice.

Wrapped in the dark taylasan, she slipped into the corridor. Being on the move relaxed her, and with a sure step, she started toward the animal pens. It was the only path Aminah knew, and when she arrived, she found the great cavern empty of thieves. *They must be sleeping,* she thought. *Or eating, perhaps.*

In the perpetual darkness of the Citadel, Aminah had lost track of time. Was it day or night? Were the men sleeping or away on another raid? She decided they must be sleeping. Otherwise, someone would be tending to the animals.

Unable to believe she was truly alone, Aminah stood at the top of the great stone staircase looking down on the stalls and listening for a human voice. Most of the torches had been extinguished, bathing the cavern in what passed for dusk in this underground world. The darkness—and her fear—seemed to heighten her senses. She strained to pick up any hint of danger, but only soft animal noises reached her ears.

Aminah turned her face toward the array of darkened corridors that branched in several directions. She glided to each entrance, lowering her hood to better sense the draft she'd noticed earlier. To her disappointment, a light breeze flowed into each opening. She'd hoped to follow a single river of air to the way out.

Well, then, she thought, *perhaps I can go the way I came.* Aminah remembered the strange words the driver had uttered to open a path through the water. She had repeated them until they were firmly lodged in her head. But before trying the incantation, she had to find Omar.

Aminah knew the direction of the kitchen from watching Iron Toe lead Omar away, and she was certain the cook's quarters would not be far from his scullery. She moved quickly down the corridor Iron Toe had taken. Soon it took a turn and opened into a filthy dining hall, littered with bones and crusts of bread. Aminah guessed Hammarab himself didn't take his meals here. She skirted the low tables and greasy cushions and found the kitchen at the far side.

Though air currents vented the smoke up and out of the cavern through natural flues, the heat was still stifling. As she entered the scullery, Aminah reached up to throw back her hood, but instead she reversed course, suddenly bending her head and pulling the heavy woolen cowl lower.

A boy—the same boy she already knew—crouched before a fire pit, stirring a deep cauldron. He started at Aminah's gasp, dropping his long spoon into the bubbling mess. He gaped fearfully at the hooded figure as the spoon sank from sight. "I—I— I'll fish it out," he stammered, wiping the sleep from his eyes. Jumping up, he reached for a meat hook. "I can do it quick."

Aminah waved off his fear and, deepening her voice, muttered a single word: "Omar?"

The boy grew limp at his imagined reprieve, and he happily pointed the way. She left him dragging the bottom of the pot with his hook and soon found Omar curled up in the corner of a storeroom. He lay on a straw pallet, so still he might have been dead, and her heart skipped a beat. But then his eyes flew open.

"Aminah!" he whispered. "I was just on my way to find you. Is the boy still awake?"

"You were coming for me? Where is everyone, Omar?" she asked, suddenly wary. "How is it you're free to move about?"

"Is he asleep?" he asked again.

"No."

Omar shook his head. "I don't understand."

Impatient with this senseless conversation, Aminah put a finger to her lips and motioned him to follow. She had a hand on his arm and felt him stiffen at the sight of the boy.

She prodded him in the back, and from the depths of her cowl, she growled out three words: "To Iron Toe." The boy shivered at the name and riveted his gaze on the cauldron.

Aminah insisted Omar not speak as they hurried up the corridor. "There may be another kitchen boy about," she whispered.

When they reached the staircase, Omar surveyed the deserted cavern with a smug look. She urged him forward, and they crept down the steps and past the stalls, approaching the Citadel's entrance.

"I remember the words that part the waters," said Omar. "Do you?"

"I wouldn't have come here if I didn't," she answered.

"Well, then, you may have the honor of saying them."

"So kind of you," Aminah replied with a grim smile.

The entrance had little need of a guard, and, indeed, no one was there. A wall of water towered above them, held back by an invisible force. It shimmered in the light of a single torch.

Aminah raised her arms in the same manner as the wagon driver had done and called out: "Sea of Darkness, in the name of Julnar receive us!"

"You're a smart one, I see. But not smart enough."

They whirled about to see Iron Toe stepping from behind a boulder. His peg rapped out a rhythm as he drew near enough to press the tip of a scimitar into Omar's chest. "It requires different words, you see. Different words to open the waters from below."

eleven

IRON TOE BOUND Omar's hands before herding him and Aminah back up the staircase. Despair weighed down her step, and she stumbled on several stairs.

"Where are all the others?" Aminah asked dully. "Where is Hammarab? I demand to see him."

Iron Toe laughed. "Demand, do you? Well, you will face him soon enough."

When they reached her apartment, Aminah was pushed inside and the door bolted. "Where are you taking Omar?" she cried before Iron Toe's scarred face disappeared, but the old pirate didn't answer. She kicked at the bronze door and then turned on it yet again with her fists. But the raw flesh of her hands caused Aminah to cry out.

Defeated, she sat, leaning against the cold bronze, and cradled her head. Despair took her again, but rather than fueling her rage, it left her feeling wasted. Her eyelids drooped.

Aminah had barely drifted into fitful slumber when the heavy door moved her forward. Dazed, she rolled to the side as Hammarab peered around the edge. Then he eased open the bronze slab until it was wide enough to enter.

"I hear you have been adventurous in my absence," he said, motioning for her to stand.

She stared at him, wary of the calmness in his voice.

Hammarab's eyes locked on the strips of cloth wrapping each of her hands. Aminah looked down and saw the crimson stains that had caught his attention. "You wished so badly to escape me?" he asked.

"No one wishes to be captive," she answered quietly.

Hammarab's lips compressed into a tight line, and he grasped her arm. "Come," he said, pulling her from the apartment.

Bewildered by fatigue, Aminah could never have retraced their steps. Hammarab guided her around corners lit by smoky torchlight until they stood before another set of bronze doors. With little more than a touch, they swung inward without a noise, and Aminah saw a room more sumptuous than her own. Amid the sparkling mosaics that decorated the walls—a hunting scene on one side, a garden scene on the other—she spied a low table spread with delicacies only a caravan could have provided.

"Has Omar returned to the kitchen?" she dared ask.

"He prepared this meal before your attempted escape," answered the thief lord.

Several wicker birdcages hung about the room, filling the

place with the sounds of fluttering, chirping, and flutelike song. A ruby-throated bird Aminah didn't recognize trilled a melodious tune over and over again, and for a moment, the music soothed her troubled heart.

Inexplicably, a clear fount sprang from the garden scene, cascading down a rock ledge protruding from the wall and into a crevice in the floor. The chatter of falling water joined with birdsong, creating an illusion that made one forget the mountain suspended overhead. Hammarab smiled at the obvious effect the room was having on Aminah.

"My refuge from the rigors of cavern life. Sit," he ordered, with a gesture toward the table.

As she obeyed, a servant appeared with a basin and ewer, and she held out her hands for ritual washing. Hammarab dampened her fingers, avoiding the bandages.

"In the name of Allah," he said, draping a napkin across his knees.

Aminah's head jolted up at the thought of a murderer calling upon God. But she immediately dropped her eyes and repeated his brief blessing.

She wondered afterward if the twittering of finches had beguiled her—or if her food had been laced with some sort of calming agent—so dulled were her anxieties. Or perhaps she was overcome by despair to the point of withdrawal. Whatever the reason, Aminah couldn't remain alert. She struggled to stay in the conversation as they ate, only giving brief answers to his casual questions.

"We have gotten on well enough, don't you think?" Hammarab asked as the servant cleared the dishes. "After all, you and I are cut from the same cloth. And so I will give you one last opportunity to save yourself—and your uncle. I should have killed him on the spot, you know, even though you likely put him up to it."

Aminah stirred from her reverie. "Kill him?" she asked. "For trying to escape at my bidding?"

Hammarab pounded a fist into the table, and Aminah fell back with a cry. "For poisoning my men!" he shouted. "For poisoning me, had I not been away with a small troop. Don't play the idiot—you know very well what he did."

"Yes," she said, thinking rapidly. "I—I suggested the plan while we were still in the wagon. Uncle Omar was reluctant, but I convinced him." She paused, her face ashen. "Are . . . are they dead?"

Hammarab's look was puzzled. "No. He only drugged them. I found the whole Citadel asleep when I returned—all but Iron Toe and the boy. Neither of them ate the tainted food—the boy because he was being punished and Iron Toe because, well, because he's Iron Toe. Did you instruct Omar to kill us all? Am I to believe he had mercy on us by choosing a sleeping powder instead?"

"You really believe I'd kill so easily?" asked Aminah, unable to keep the scorn from her voice. "We are nothing alike, you and I. Yes, we spent our childhoods in a similar manner, but what we took from our days on the street sent us in opposite directions."

"Are you so certain?" he asked.

"Yes," she answered, daring to challenge the danger in his voice.

Hammarab exploded to his feet, rounding the table and pulling Aminah up. He took her by the shoulders and drew her close. She steeled herself for the revulsion of his lips against hers, but he only held her close for a moment, whispering into her ear. "You can never leave here alive, as you know the secret for entering the Citadel. So, stay with me or die. As you've discovered, escape is impossible."

He released her and strode to the door. "Oh," he said, turning. "One more thing. Allow us to be fed without fear, or Omar dies. On the other hand, perhaps I'll keep him and dispense with you. A good cook is worth his weight in gold. You have until tomorrow to decide."

"Then allow me to spend the rest of my time with Omar," she said.

Hammarab's eyes narrowed, but then he shrugged. "Perhaps he will help you to make the right decision."

He clapped his hands, and two men appeared as if from nowhere. "She will abide with the cook until I call for her," Hammarab said, and as they led her away, he spoke again. "Keep your hands to yourselves, boys. For now, at least."

The thieves herded Aminah down stairways and through stone corridors. Her head ached, and her stomach, sickened by fear and loathing, rebelled against the rich food she'd eaten. Along some dimly lit tunnel, she retched, and the men jumped back.

Cursing, they shook their puke-spattered shoes in a fruitless effort to clean them, and then dragged her forward to an iron gate the height of three men. Within the gate was a small door. One of the thieves pulled a rusty key from the pocket of his robe and unlocked it.

The space beyond the gate was as black as Azráeel's heart.

Before she could protest, the men shoved her through the opening. She landed face-first on a mound of something that scattered, clinking and clanking, into the darkness. The door creaked closed behind her, shutting out the last glimmer of torchlight.

"It is a sad day for you, friend," a voice muttered from the dark. "What have you done to deserve my fate?"

Aminah smiled. "I attempted escape, but at least I didn't poison a host of thieves."

"Aminah!" cried Omar. Another collision sent something solid bouncing across the floor. "Ow!"

A moment later, his arms encircled her, and he squeezed until she was breathless. "Did he hurt you?" he asked, releasing her.

"No," Aminah gasped.

"That is good. I was worried."

"But he'll hurt both of us, unless I consent to stay with him. Or he may keep you and get rid of me."

"Never!" Omar flung himself away from her, and she heard him strike something with such force that it landed far away in the darkness. He stifled a moan, and Aminah imagined him cradling a battered hand. "Oh, but for a moment with my magic," he whispered.

"At least we're together for a while. Perhaps we'll think of another plan as fine as your last one. It almost worked, Omar. Where did you find the sleeping powder?"

"It was among the booty taken from the caravan. Oh, that it had been a deadly poison instead."

"You don't mean that," she said, edging in the direction of

his voice. Her foot struck another mound, setting off an avalanche. She reached down, taking up a handful of the scree. "Coins," she said.

"Yes. This is one of Hammarab's treasure rooms."

"But . . . what about Gindar?" Aminah asked.

"You would think a treasure trove would be to his liking," Omar answered. "But I have discovered something strange about . . ."

His words trailed off. Aminah heard the tinkling of coins and trinkets running through his fingers, and her stomach tightened. "Something strange, you say? Tell me about it," she prompted, hoping to distract him from the treasure.

"A miracle!" he cried. "A treasure worth more to us than gold!"

"Fight him!" she shouted. "Don't let Gindar take you!"

Omar laughed. "Do not fret—I am still here."

"Don't do that," Aminah grumbled. "You frightened me."

"My deepest apologies," he said. "But you will forgive my Gindar-like exuberance for treasure, that I can promise. I am very near an object of power, you see. Though I am bereft of magic, I can nevertheless sense enchantments. It is a small thing—very small—but I will know it by touch."

"Will it help us escape?"

"Yes."

Omar continued rummaging through the layers of plunder, but soon he began grunting with displeasure. "Chalices, platters, trinkets, baubles—I could search for days. Aha!"

"You found it!"

"A ring," said Omar. "Ordinary in decoration by the feel of it, but I believe it may be the ring of a jinni."

"Give it to me," Aminah demanded. She flailed her arms, searching for him, but Omar found her and pressed the ring into her hand.

She stood in the dark, confused. "Why isn't Gindar here?" she asked. "Why hasn't he come to load his pockets with gold?"

"Treasure seems to have no hold on Gindar, if he cannot see it," Omar answered. "That is my strange discovery. Go on, rub the ring."

With quivering fingers, she stroked it, as she would have the lamp, hungry for its magic. But the ring, cool to the touch, lay dormant in her palm. Then something shifted as she traced its surface with her finger.

"There's a small disk mounted on the ring," she said breathlessly. "It turns." The disk clicked as she rotated it.

For what seemed like hours, they huddled over the ring, moving the disk this way and that. First, they tried three rotations to the right—then to the left. The patterns were endless, and with each one, Omar suggested a variety of commands: "Jinni appear! Come forth, slave of the ring! Demon, show thyself!"

At long last, their patience exhausted, they crouched sullenly in the dark. "You of all people should know about such things," Aminah complained. "Have you lost your memory as well as your magic? Put your mind to it, demon!"

"It has been a long while since you last addressed me in that way—at least in that tone," said Omar. "However, it is not you who speaks, but rather your own demons."

Aminah fought the urge to scream. "I'm so wild to be away from here! Sometimes I think I'll die if I'm separated from the lamp a moment longer."

Omar touched her arm. "I have seen the effects of magic twist the guts of more than one human in my day. Once, I derived great pleasure from it—but not so with you, Aminah. Not with you."

Aminah felt for Omar's hand and held it tightly. "So, you knew this would happen. Why didn't you warn me?"

"You seemed unaffected until the lamp disappeared. The occasional flare-up, perhaps, and I assumed it was your good heart that made you immune. Indeed, it has protected you. A lesser human would have lost her mind by now—considering how you have used the lamp. Never has a master plied its magic so often and with such intensity. Actually, you are quite a marvel."

"I don't feel like one," she said.

As Aminah gave his hand a desperate squeeze, Omar cleared his throat. "As it seems we may meet our end in this place, I must confess an old misdeed. Do you recall the rule about wishing for powers?"

"Of course. If I lose the lamp to another, then magic powers you granted to me vanish—even if I wished them for another, such as Ahab the tailor. But a magic tool, such as my money box, I can keep."

"Well, I lied," he said. "A jinni may choose *not* to take back such powers. There! I feel so much better, getting that nasty little secret off my chest."

Aminah sat in dazed silence. "You serpent!" she cried at last. "How many wishes did we waste during those last days in Al-Kal'as? You remember how the lamp was of necessity passed from me to Idris—and then to Barra? And each time we wasted wishes restoring Ahab's magical tailoring skills—and Hassan's baking talents—when you might have chosen to leave them intact."

"But it is you who forget," said Omar. "Idris gave back Ahab's skills and some of Hassan's powers. Then the lamp was passed to Barra to do the rest—including bringing us to Tyre. According to the rule, Ahab's gifts would have disappeared again the moment Barra became the lamp's master."

Aminah groaned. "Why didn't I remember that would happen? And of course, you didn't bother to remind me. Oh, Omar, why do you make things so difficult? But wait! As I recall, Hassan didn't lose the powers Idris had wished for him."

"Yes, I chose not to take them back when the lamp's master changed—and I tell you, that is almost unheard of in the jinn world. I allowed Ahab to keep his gifts as well. A bit of a jinni humor, I suppose, to let you think otherwise."

Aminah scowled in the darkness. "The jinn have no sense of humor, as far as I can see."

"Or perhaps I believed the irritation of repeating the wishes for Ahab and Hassan would convince you to take back the lamp—to become my master again. Bear in mind, you had decided to give me over to Barra once and for all."

"Yes—mostly because of this sort of behavior." She sighed deeply. "Once again I must wonder if you can ever really be trusted. Why, you even pretended to be giddy from all your good deeds that day."

"No, I was not pretending. I was truly—" Omar stopped, and Aminah heard him jump to his feet, sending treasure flying. "I am an addlepated fool!" he cried. "Put the ring on your finger!"

Stunned by his outburst, Aminah was slow to move. Omar felt for the ring and plucked it from her grasp. Then he slipped it over her thumb. "Now, we must try again."

They started back through every pattern—rotating the disk and calling out commands—but the results were no better.

"I was certain wearing the ring was the key," he said.

"What do we do now?" Aminah asked, unhappily twisting the ring in circles around her thumb. Though she wasn't counting, after the third revolution there was a change, and Omar sensed it.

"Something is happening, is it not?"

"It's warm—no, it's hot! I can't get it off!"

Omar tried to twist the ring free. The fire inside was building, and soon it would sear her flesh. But in the next instant, the heat dissipated, and the ring began to glow with a cold light. They were bathed in its sickly green aura.

A choking stench wafted over them, and Aminah gagged. The source of the foul odor was a shriveled form that had materialized in a puff of putrid green smoke. He stood before them, barely visible in the dull glow he radiated. He was dressed in filthy rags and reeking with the scent of the unwashed.

"Oh mighty Master," the emaciated creature whined. "Expect little from one such as I. Weak—yes, weak, be Sixer." He launched into a coughing fit, and his head exploded, only to reappear on his left shoulder.

"A four-digit jinni," Omar whispered, wrinkling his nose. "The smell alone reveals the fact."

The demon's neck extended, bringing his head to within a hand's span of Omar's nose. "And why know you of jinn's digits? Unless . . ." He clapped a filthy hand on Omar's shoulder and closed his eyes. "No, you be without magic," he said at last. "But not without insults! How be it you ken the demon world?"

"I myself was one of the jinn," Omar replied, puffing out his chest. "Still am, I suppose. You might say I am on temporary leave. How is it you have a name, Sixer? Jinn do not have names."

"Free from ring or lamp, you say? No, such cannot occur. Yet, none but demon could know such things."

"Tell me about your name," Omar urged.

Sixer's head popped to his right shoulder, closer to Aminah. He peered at her through pale eyes the color of pus. "You be the master. Should I respond?"

"Not that old trick," said Aminah. "You plan to count my answer as a wish."

The jinni blinked several times in surprise, then sputtered, "N-n-not so. Not so, I say!"

"My digit is 4-8," said Omar. "No name—a number only."

"A two-digit jinni?" said Sixer warily. "Why ought I trust a two-digit demon? They be nasty to my kind."

Though they couldn't make out each other's face in the dim light, Aminah threw Omar a sharp look. Feeling rather than seeing her disapproval, he answered in a lofty tone, "You would not understand. It is the way of things."

"Well, he can't hurt you now," she said to the imp. "No magic."

Sixer thought about this for a moment, and then his face creased in what Aminah thought might be a smile. "Yes, no magic. No magic for the magnificent Mr. 4-8, who thinks himself so superior to 66-66. Poor, lowly four-digit 66-66. It be the likes of you who burdened me with the tag of Sixer—so many sixes, says he. Too many to remember, says he, and so he calls me Sixer. But once I was three-digit. Oh, them were the days," he murmured dreamily, then turned on Omar with a frightening scowl. "Until the likes of you ruined me!"

"My guess is you ruined yourself," Omar shot back. "Whatever you did to be demoted to four digits—well, I cannot make myself think of it."

"See! See! Now I know you be demon—only a hard-hearted, two-digit jinni would say such things! You think you be so exalted—"

"You act no better than you smell!" shouted Omar. "I earned my number, just as you certainly earned yours."

Sixer growled, sounding so much like a mad dog that Aminah cringed. "What are your rules for wish making?" she asked quickly.

"What be that you ask?" Sixer's head swiveled in her direction. "No human—I say, no human asks such a thing."

"This one does," said Omar. "And I tell you, it once befuddled me, too."

"The rules, the rules!" Sixer howled.

"Stalling won't help you," said Aminah. "Tell me the rules now—and don't try to make a wish out of it."

"Yes, why not tell? It cannot hurt for you to know. I am a cursed, lesser, four-digit jinni," he said, with a nasty glance at

Omar. "I have only three wishes to grant any one master—three and that be all. And know this: there be no trading the ring back and forth among friends. Use your wishes, and then cast the ring away, for it be of no use to you and yours."

"The rules are clear," said Aminah, "so I will make my first wish. I wish you to transport 4-8 and me to Al-Kal'as. Set us down without harm just outside the main city gate."

"That will require two wishes," he answered with a wicked grin.

"No, it doesn't. You can move things by classes—all people, all horses. Who do you think you're dealing with, demon?"

Sixer's grin slid into a sneer. "I be the slave between thy palms," he said, bowing. He clapped his hands and disappeared, and with him went the light.

"This does not look like Al-Kal'as," said Omar. "Unless we have arrived during an exceptionally dark night."

Aminah was about to summon Sixer again, but the familiar, icy pinpricks on her arms stopped her. "Brace yourself," she said, and in the next instant the treasure room was deserted.

True to her wish, she stood before the gates of Al-Kal'as, Omar at her side. "We did it!" she cried. "We're free!"

Aminah turned in a happy circle, until her eyes fell on the city wall. She slowed to a stop, trembling, and stared at its pink stones, which had turned a deeper rose color in the light of the setting sun. But whether she trembled in fear of Badr or in nervous anticipation of regaining the lamp, Aminah was uncertain.

She turned to Omar, and at the sight of him, her already unsteady knees gave way. She fell in the dust, gaping in horror. The man next to her wore Omar's clothing, but not his face. Unpleasant, beady eyes stared back at her, and a bristled snout, framed by Omar's beard, wrinkled in a puzzled grin.

She had arrived in Al-Kal'as with a pig.

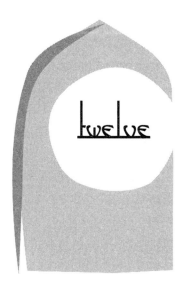

twelve

OMAR WHIRLED AROUND to see what had frightened Aminah, but he saw nothing more than a bent old man leading a donkey. He turned back to her, raising his hands. "What?" he asked, and his eyes widened at the grunting noise that had escaped his lips. His hands flew to his face, and as he touched his new snout, Omar screamed. What Aminah heard was a high-pitched squeal.

He dropped to the ground beside her. "Sixer!" he grunted, grinding his porcine teeth. "That demon scum will be five-digit—no, six-digit—when I am finished with him!"

Omar's shrill grunting had drawn the attention of a small band of travelers approaching the gate. "Quick, shroud your face," said Aminah, thrusting a heavy scarf into his hands. His snout contorted in disgust, but he swathed his head with loose wraps of silk until only his small, round eyes showed.

"An unclean beast," Omar moaned. "The filthy little imp has cursed me with the worst of creatures."

"Come," said Aminah. "I know a place to hide."

Under the watchful gaze of the Sultan's Guard, she led him through the massive city gate. There was no reason for the guards to single them out, but Aminah held her breath until they were safely past. As a beggar girl, she had run for her life from the guards of Al-Kal'as, and the mere sight of them now reawakened her old fears. But she controlled the impulse to bolt and calmly steered Omar toward her old hideaway.

Aminah had thought to stay in a khan as normal travelers did, but sneaking Omar past the innkeeper would be too big a risk. Besides, they didn't have money for a khan. She had forgotten to borrow from Hammarab's treasure, except for a few of the golden trinkets she had absentmindedly dropped in her pocket. Of course, Aminah knew she could sell the trinkets—two of them were set with diamonds and ought to bring a good price—but that would take time.

Once out of the guards' sight, they moved rapidly through the narrow streets, jostling passersby. A few protested—until they met Omar's gaze. Unnerved by feral eyes peering from the folds of silk, they stepped aside in silence.

The sun had dipped below the rooftops when Aminah pulled Omar down an alley. Stopping before a rusted iron gate, she probed a slit in the stone near one of the hinges and withdrew two sharp iron slivers. "They're still here," she said with obvious satisfaction.

A moment later she had picked the well-oiled lock. She

ushered Omar into a narrow corridor that lay between a building and the outer wall of Al-Kal'as. But for the tiny space where they stood, it was choked with stacks of rubbish: splintered crates, broken furniture, cracked storage jars. A doorway at the opposite end was partly visible behind the teetering piles.

"Dusk will mask our climb," Aminah said.

"Climb? Where are you taking me?"

"To the top of the city wall," she answered, sliding her foot into a knee-high crevice. But as she pushed herself up, her fingers finding another crevice above her head, the corridor was flooded with light.

"Marhaba?" It was a girl's voice. Her slight form was silhouetted in the yellow glow from the open door. She held a clay lamp aloft, illuminating her face and reflecting light from her large, dark eyes.

"Hello?" she said again. "Who's there? Oh, I see you now."

She pulled the door closed and wended her way through the rubbish. Aminah was startled by the girl's complete lack of fear and would have thought her dim-witted but for the clear, intelligent sound of her voice.

Omar fought to open the gate as the girl advanced. Though its lock was oiled, its latch was rusted and suddenly stubborn. Aminah tugged at his robe. "Wait," she whispered. "She would have called out to her father had she wished us harm."

The girl sidestepped the last obstacle in her path and drew near. "What have you done to your hands?" she asked. She set the lamp on a battered crate and took one of Aminah's hands in hers. "You're still bleeding. I'll get salve and fresh bandages."

Aminah reached out to stop her. "What is your name?"

The girl smiled. "I am Barra, but my mother called me Sparrow. I think it's because I flit about like a little bird." Indeed, she couldn't seem to stay still, bobbing her head and shifting from one foot to the other.

Aminah glanced at Omar, whose tiny eyes widened. "I know another Barra," she said. "Someone dear to me. Your name is a good omen—that and you seem not to fear us."

"I usually trust people," said Sparrow. "Father used to say I'm foolish, that a ten-year-old like me—only I was nine back then—ought to have more wisdom. I suppose he was right, but I'm not so trusting as to open the door to thieves. I heard a girl's voice, and I liked its sound. Now I see you have kind eyes, though I can't say as much for your friend." She knelt as she spoke, picking through a jumble of old jars and sorting out the good ones. Indeed, she reminded Aminah of a tiny sparrow pecking at flower seeds.

"What's *your* name?" the girl asked, looking up.

"Aminah. And this is my Uncle Omar."

Omar bowed, and the silk wrapping slipped, revealing his snout. Sparrow gasped and jumped up for a closer look. Omar quickly covered his face.

Aminah put a bandaged hand on Sparrow's shoulder, feeling the constant movement in her small body. Telling the girl at least some of the truth seemed the best option, and so she said, "He's been enchanted. It's part of the reason we're hiding. The other part is a longer story."

"Then he's not really a swine?" Sparrow asked, and Aminah shook her head. "Enchantments! I've always believed in magic, though Father said it's foolish to. Was it an evil sorcerer?"

Sparrow was bouncing under Aminah's touch, and she pressed down to steady her. "A jinni," she answered.

"Even better!" the girl exclaimed. "How can I help?"

"You can help by not giving us away," said Aminah.

"Of course I won't give you away," Sparrow said. "This is the most exciting thing to ever happen to me—enchantments! Besides, if I help you, maybe you can help me. I can do more than keep a secret, you know. Stay here, and I'll bring food— Mr. Omar looks starved—and medicine for your hands."

"Sparrow, my uncle and I are in danger. We can't risk being found, yet now you've found us. We must go. Our staying wouldn't be safe for you."

"No!" Sparrow cried. "Please don't go. Or at least, if you do, take me with you."

Aminah took the girl by the shoulders. "What's wrong, Barra?"

Sparrow shrugged. "I have an uncle, too. He doesn't look like a pig, but he acts like one. Sorry, Mr. Omar."

"Then your parents . . ."

Sparrow nodded. "Maybe if I'd had a sister—even a brother—things would be different. Look, you don't really have to take me with you, but please let me help. Wait here; I'll be right back. By the way, were you climbing the wall?"

Aminah sighed. "Yes. I have an old hiding place up there."

"Wait here," Sparrow repeated, and taking the lamp, she threaded her way to the door and disappeared.

"Do you trust the girl?" Omar grunted.

"Yes. Somehow I think she needs us, even if it's just for a little while."

When the door opened again, the house was dark. Sparrow still carried the clay lamp, and as she picked her way toward them, Aminah could see she also carried a heavy-laden bag.

"Uncle is out," she said, "so I had no trouble getting what you need." Sparrow handed Aminah the lamp and then pulled a jar of salve and strips of linen from the bag, which she tossed to Omar.

Aminah held the lamp close to Sparrow's face to get a better look at her and sucked in her breath at the angry bruise near the girl's left eye.

"I can't seem to do much that pleases him," was all the girl would say.

"Oh, Sparrow," murmured Aminah, her throat suddenly constricted. "I can't help you now, but I'll be back. I promise."

"I believe you," she said.

As the girl unwrapped Aminah's sore hands and applied the salve, Omar snorted with satisfaction as he emptied the bag of its bread, cheese, and roasted lamb. He stuffed his mouth greedily.

"By the way," Sparrow said as she worked, "I think you make a perfectly lovely boar. As fine-looking a boar as I've ever laid eyes on."

Omar blinked, unsure whether or not this was a compliment.

"I only say that in case you can't get the spell reversed," she said. "You ought to know you're handsome all the same."

"Shukra," Omar grunted.

"You're welcome," she answered, tying off the last of the new bandages. "Keep the salve jar, Aminah. Here are extra linen strips for later."

"We are in your debt, Sparrow, but won't your uncle miss what you've taken?" asked Aminah.

The girl shook her head. "He's closefisted, it's true, and

you'd think he'd notice what's missing. But Uncle hoards so much of everything"—she waggled her fingers at the piles of junk surrounding them—"that he can't keep up with anything."

Aminah smiled at Sparrow's assessment of her uncle, and then she said, "I must get Omar settled. Then perhaps you can point me toward the nearest suq." Although Aminah already knew the way, she wanted Sparrow to feel useful.

"But most stalls in the marketplace will be shut up for the night. Is it more food you need?"

"No, Sparrow, what you've given us is enough," said Aminah. "The suq teems with information, and that's what I seek. Come, Uncle Omar, follow me up the wall."

Aminah was halfway to the top when she looked back to see Omar still standing on the ground. "It's not as difficult as it looks," she said. "You'll have perfect grip. Whoever carved out these crevices made certain of that."

"We pigs are not known for climbing," Omar grunted. "Better I stay here."

"It's not safe. What if Sparrow's uncle should find you? Until I locate Idris—and that may take a few days—you'll need a place to stay."

"And I'll bring you food," offered Sparrow.

"Just try a few handholds before giving up," Aminah urged, grateful that Sixer's curse hadn't changed Omar's hands into trotters.

He tossed his head like an enraged boar and kicked the toe of his boot into the lowest crevice. Snorting, he reached for the first handhold and was surprised to find that his fingers folded around what felt like a handle. Though darkness had shrouded the alley, he discovered he didn't need his eyes; his hands and feet seemed to slip into the crevices instinctively as he worked his way upward.

Aminah tugged on his robe as he reached the top and helped him over the edge. He lay back, squealing with glee. "I did it!" he said, sitting up. "And look at this! A spectacular view: the desert, the Sultan's palace, the suq! You actually lived here?"

Aminah nodded. "But my memories aren't pleasant. I was always a day or two away from starving to death—this would likely have been my tomb but for the lamp."

"There are worse places to die," said Omar, surveying the city at his feet. "But I am pleased to have snatched you from Azráeel's clutches."

Aminah smiled. "The night you first appeared to me, you couldn't have cared less whether or not the Angel of Death carried me away."

"More than my face has changed since that time."

"Yes, you've become a good friend, Jinni, and I choose not to lose you to Gindar. I will have the lamp again, no matter the cost." She thought wistfully of all the things she could fix with a little magic: Hassan's broken body, Jinni's face, Ella's troubles, and now Sparrow's unhappy life. "Wait here for me," she said.

"Jinni?" Sparrow's head popped above the edge of the wall. "Is that who he really is? Have you lost his magic lamp? Are you here to find it? Did this Gindar steal it?"

Aminah gaped at the girl's moonlit features. "You are a smart one," she said, and then realized with a grim smile that she'd just quoted Iron Toe. "If a bit nosy," she added. "You shouldn't have been listening."

"A real jinni! This gets better and better!"

"Start down, Sparrow. Direct me to the suq." Though Aminah's heart told her the girl wasn't a threat, she still was uncomfortable with her knowing so much.

As confident as though she had wings, Sparrow flew down the rock face. Aminah slid over the edge and stopped. "I may be a while. Get some rest," she said to Omar.

"You cannot do this alone," he said. "Sixer! I call down the foulest curses on his flea-bitten head!" He paused, an odd grin curling his snout. "What fools we are! There is an easy answer. Summon the maggot and command him to undo his handiwork."

"I can't do that," said Aminah.

"Yes, yes! You can," Omar squealed.

"No, I have but two wishes remaining. We'll likely need them to succeed—and escape. When I have the lamp, you can fix yourself. I'm sorry. I hate to see you like this, but it would be foolish to waste our best chance to make it home safely."

Omar stared in sad disbelief. "Go then," he whispered hoarsely. "I see you do not need me."

"We can't afford the time to argue," she said. "You'll see I'm right about this. Sixer may prove to be our only hope—the difference between life and death. I'll return before dawn, so don't worry. I'm only going out to listen for gossip. Don't forget, you have Sparrow's bag."

Omar's drooping ears perked up at the memory of food, and drool began to trickle from the corners of his mouth. "Away with you, then," he said. "The sooner you go, the sooner you return."

Taking advantage of his improved spirits, Aminah was on the ground before Omar could wipe his chin. Sparrow had worked on the latch, and the gate stood open. Hopping about with excitement, she led Aminah from the alley into the street. "Now we go this way," she said, starting forward.

"No, Sparrow. Your uncle may come home and find you missing. I must go alone—just give me directions."

The girl started to protest, but Aminah took her hands. "Check on Omar, if you can. And don't let your uncle catch you. Please, do this for me."

Sparrow nodded. She mumbled directions to the suq and then stood watching until Aminah rounded a corner, disappearing from sight.

With fewer people about, Aminah moved with speed and purpose, glancing back now and again to be certain Sparrow wasn't trailing behind. The streets were, in some strange way, no longer quite like she recalled. However, the alleyways were still the dark tunnels she remembered, and knowing their potential dangers, she traveled the main thoroughfares. Soon the welcome noise of a crowd reached her ears.

Aminah turned the final corner and entered the suq, which was illuminated by a great numbers of lamps and torches. It was one of the few marketplaces in Al-Kal'as that was busy into the late hours, and it was the best place to pick up the latest news.

She straightened her clothing and washed her hands and face in the wide fountain at the suq's center. Then Aminah surveyed the marketplace and was pleased to find the stall of a gold merchant open for business. She decided to sell Hammarab's trinkets before searching for Idris.

She was relieved when the merchant didn't question her. She must have appeared sufficiently respectable, for he didn't so much as lift an eyebrow when she offered the tiny gold pieces for sale. He bought them for half of what they were worth. Aminah had expected no more than that, and so she was pleased.

Next, she purchased a pomegranate from one of the fruit vendors who hadn't yet closed shop, and then settled down by the fountain to eat and listen. By day, storytellers and snake charmers—or perhaps a troupe of musicians or a trainer with acrobatic monkeys—would be found where she sat, but at night, people gathered in this place to visit. As she nibbled on the ruby-red seeds, Aminah gathered in the bits of conversation that washed over her, sifting through them for the right words.

"Life in Al-Kal'as has improved with Aladdin in the Sultan's seat," someone said. "Don't you agree?"

"Yes, indeed," came the answer.

At the sound of Aladdin's name, Aminah lowered the pomegranate and turned to find two men, their beards graying, sitting on the low and protruding edge of the fountain. A game of backgammon was balanced between them.

"In fact, I haven't missed the old fellow once—not once, I tell you, since the day he died," said the old man closest to her. "Now, if that daughter of his had stayed away, I'd be predicting a bright future. As it is, I'm not so sure. Word is she resents her husband and would have her father's position for her own."

The game pieces lay idle as the other man considered this. Finally, he shook his head. "No, she is only a woman. Aladdin is certainly the master of his wife."

No, he is not, Aminah said to herself.

"But we should be thankful she was not a son—that there

were no sons at all," he continued. "Aladdin is a man of the people, as no sultan's spawn could be."

Now Aminah realized why the streets seemed less familiar. No beggar had reached out to slow her progress. She glanced about the suq, locating only three men with their hands out, and they were not working the crowd. Instead, they hovered at the perimeter of the torchlight. During her time on the streets, there would have been ten or twenty times as many in this one spot. *Aladdin must be feeding the poor,* she thought. *Or perhaps he's found something useful for them to do.*

As for the news about Badr, Aminah hadn't held out much hope that the Princess would still be in Makkah. Nevertheless, it sent a shiver through her just to know with certainty that she and Badr shared the same air. How long had the Princess been home? And how long would it take her to put an end to Aladdin's foolish generosity?

From experience, Aminah knew that the rumor about Badr's lust for power was true; she had heard as much from the Princess's own lips. The Full Moon of Full Moons planned to rule in her father's stead, and for that she needed the lamp.

Aminah drew a scarf over her face and edged closer to the old men. "Forgive me," she said. "I am searching for someone—a storyteller. He is a young man but very talented. Do you know him?"

"A friend? Or perhaps someone dearer?" asked the closer of the two, his eyes twinkling.

"My brother," she answered.

"I may know something," said the other. "For the price of that pomegranate, my knowledge is yours."

"Stop it, Hammud, you old goat."

"A joke, Khalid. Just a joke," said Hammud. He grinned, showing numerous gaps amid his stained teeth. "We hear the Sultan's court employs a young storyteller. He resides in the palace, or so it's said."

"He lives with the Sultan? But . . . but that's not possible. He would never . . . ." Aminah hesitated. "His name?" she asked, her voice tight. "Do you know his name?"

"Yes, little one," said Khalid. "But my friend has not been forthcoming. This young man has quite a reputation. Everyone in Al-Kal'as knows him."

"Again, can you name him?"

"Idris," he answered.

thirteen

AMINAH LEFT THE POMEGRANATE rocking to and fro in the center of the backgammon board. As she raced back to Omar, a small shadow fell in next to her, joining her stride for stride.

"Sparrow!"

"You knew the way without my instructions," the girl said. "I could tell by the sureness of your step. Which makes sense, if you lived here long enough to have a hideout on top of the wall. Who are you? Do you really know Idris? I heard him tell a story once. I believe he did it just for fun—one day as he was passing through the suq. I think he's quite handsome."

"You were to watch over Omar, not spy on me," said Aminah, quickening her pace.

Sparrow kept up easily. "Omar can take care of himself," she said. "You just wanted me out of the way. I thought you trusted me."

Aminah stopped, but Sparrow still moved, circling her with nervous energy. "I do trust you," she said, rotating to face the girl. "But I already told you—what I'm about is dangerous. I wanted to keep you from harm."

Sparrow bit her bottom lip as she weighed Aminah's words. "But I don't want to be protected," she said. "I want to help you. What if you don't let me help, and that ends up making the difference about whether or not you're around to come back for me? Helping you is helping me, don't you understand?"

Aminah studied the girl's eyes by the light of the moon. "And what if, because I allowed you to get involved, *you* aren't around to come back to? Don't worry, Sparrow," she said. "You'll see me again. Come, let's get back to Uncle Omar."

As they made their way through the streets, Aminah tried to concentrate on Sparrow's chatter, but she was distracted. Her mind worked to wrap itself around the idea that Idris was living in Badr's shadow. To think of it was painful and confusing. *Has he taken the lamp into the palace?* she wondered, and was chilled by the prospect.

Soon they turned into the alley, but as they approached the gate, Sparrow froze. "What is it?" Aminah asked.

"I locked the gate behind us," she whispered. "But look at it now." It hung askew—someone had kicked it in.

Aminah ran past the twisted sheet of metal and leapt from handhold to handhold, calling out to Omar. She didn't hear him until she was an arm's length from the top, and then the only sound was a low, guttural moan.

As she scrambled over the edge, her hand found a ragged scrap of his robe. She squinted against the night, staring at one of the battlement's merlons—the one she knew was missing several stone blocks. As an orphan, Aminah had curled up in this sizable gap to sleep, but now it held Omar's crumpled form.

He moaned again as she touched his shoulder. Then she rolled him over, gasping in unison with Sparrow. In the cloudless sky, the moon was bright enough to show a face so misshapen by beating, so bruised and swollen, that Omar looked neither human nor swine.

"They wanted gold," he muttered, teetering on the edge of sensibility. His eyes refused to focus, so he closed them. "But I was not worried, for I was confident my face would frighten them away. Instead, it only seemed to goad them. Ah, I had not remembered that pain could be so sublime."

"This looks worse than it is," said Aminah, though she trembled with uncertainty. "Before we left Tyre, you were kicked in the head by a horse—how can this compare?"

"That kick was a lover's caress by comparison," he murmured, and then drifted out of consciousness.

"I'll go for a physician," said Sparrow, her cheeks streaked with tears. "You were right, Aminah. Omar needed me. A jinni without his magic is helpless—I should have thought."

As she started away, Aminah held the tail of her robe. "Thanks to Allah you weren't with him," she said. "They would have killed you. This is not your fault, Sparrow. As for a physician, we can't very well bring him up here. I'll use your salve to treat him for now—until I can get him down. You must go now. Before your uncle comes looking."

Sparrow choked back a sob. "I don't want to leave you."

"We've been over this. Be patient. I said I'd be back for you, and I will."

With a shuddering sigh, Sparrow nodded. A moment later, she slid from sight, and when Aminah heard the door click into place, she reached for the jar of salve. Cradling Omar's battered head in her lap, she coated his wounds. She held his head through the rest of the night, dozing off only occasionally.

Whoever had followed them believed they were hiding something of great worth—and had vented their disappointment on Omar's face. *How fortunate they didn't cast him to his death,* she thought as the rounded moon waned.

Omar awakened while it was still dark and seemed to have regained some strength. "Get me down from here," he croaked. "I need water, and I have no desire to wait here for a second beating."

Aminah thought better of his making the climb, but the alternative was worse: spending a day baking in the sun. At least while it was still dark, she could find a better place to leave him before sending Sparrow for a physician. But then she realized that no one—not even a physician—must be allowed to see his porcine features. The best she could do was to seek a healer's advice.

Finding a new hiding place would not be a simple matter, and when the sun rose, things would only complicate. Aminah needed a plan before they reached the ground, and so she combed her memory for the most promising spots as she pulled Omar to his feet.

By going first and guiding his toes into the crevices, Aminah managed to get him down safely. Still, there had been some close calls—twice, his flailing boot had almost thrown her to the ground. When they reached the bottom, both were too weary to move.

As they rested, Aminah continued searching her memory for a place to go. It wasn't until Omar struggled to his feet, deciding it was time to move on, that the idea came. She would take him to her old estate. After all, she hadn't sold it. But though the house still belonged to her, would it be empty? And even if it were uninhabited, would Badr's guards nevertheless be on watch?

As she ushered Omar along the streets, he began to weaken again. To keep him conscious, she spoke to him.

"There's the spot where we first met," Aminah whispered as they passed the entrance to an alleyway. It was where she had first rubbed the tarnished lamp.

Omar's snout wrinkled. "Ah, the good old days," he mumbled.

Their journey across Al-Kal'as required more time than Aminah liked, but it was necessary to stop at regular intervals, allowing Omar to rest his wobbly legs. As they finally approached her old street, the iron-gray shroud of early dawn settled over the city.

The house was an indistinct blur in the muted light—without color or feature. Unable to see what awaited them, she dared not draw closer with Omar in tow, and yet she did not want to leave him behind. Suddenly he made the decision simple by collapsing. Aminah dropped beside him, listening for signs of life. His breathing was regular, though shallow, and so she mustered the strength to drag his inert form into a nearby alley.

After arranging Omar as comfortably as possible, Aminah

covered her face and moved back into the street. She approached the angular front gates of her estate, and as she'd suspected, they were barred. But in the increasing light, she could see that the ground in front of the gates was undisturbed. No one had passed that way for a very long time.

Encouraged, she edged along the wall until she reached the back entrance. In the past, she had seldom used this solid wooden door, sheathed in plates of iron, but she had hidden the key against the need. She removed a loose brick near the door and reached into the empty space. Her fingers probed around a corner at the end of the crevice and fished out the key.

SALADIN DEAD. Badr put out a hand to steady herself. It would be the only sign that suggested she cared. Rashid's next words banished any further thought of him.

"He had Aminah at his mercy when the arrow pierced him," Rashid said. He was unable to control the pitch of his voice when he stood in Badr's presence—it was high and tremulous and tinged with whining. She was thrilled by his fear of her, while at the same time loathing him all the more.

"You saw the girl?" Badr turned to Ashraf. "And what of the lamp, cleric?"

"She did not have it," he said, the Princess straining to hear the dry rustling of his voice. "And I did not sense its presence anywhere nearby. But our friend here may have discovered something of value."

"Aminah was . . ." For the second time, Rashid noticed Badr flinch at the name, and so he started again. "The girl was on the route to Al-Kal'as, though she was without the lamp. But she disappeared when the barbarians who killed Saladin—may Allah harbor his soul—attacked the caravans. However, at great risk, I drew near her campfire before we confronted her, and I heard her speak of someone named Idris, who had just been in Tyre. She said this Idris took 'it' from her. 'It' must have been the lamp. I asked myself, could this be the same Idris as our storyteller? But no, he was here in Al-Kal'as."

"At great risk, you say?" The Princess snorted. "Risk of what, exactly? Crawling into a thornbush while you were eaves-dropping?"

Rashid stared at the floor.

Badr's face darkened. "The storyteller left the city before you returned from your search for the coffer. He traveled to Damascus to visit his dying mother."

Rashid's eyes came up. "He has no mother. He was orphaned as a young boy."

Badr cried out and ripped away a drapery near at hand. Palpable waves of anger forced everyone to step back—even Ashraf.

"Faysal!" She spat the name with such venom that the man hesitated before answering.

"Yes, oh effulgent one," he said, head bowed.

"You are now Captain of the Guard. I shall arrange it with . . . the Sultan. I know you are as loyal to me, and to me alone, as was Saladin, but I wish to hear as much. Do you pledge in Allah's name to serve me above all others?"

Ashraf glanced up at Badr, his eyes registering surprise that she would dare include Allah in her oath.

"To die for my cause, if necessary?" she continued. "And do you pledge secrecy in fulfilling my purposes?"

"In the name of God, I swear these things, oh Full Moon of Full Moons."

"Then, Faysal, you *shall* answer to God," said Ashraf. With a nod in the Princess's direction, he slid past the two eunuchs guarding the door and disappeared from the room. Badr ignored his unexcused departure.

"Captain," she said, "my husband's head is among the clouds. He is so preoccupied with his latest project—emptying the swill in Beggars' Corridor—that he notices nothing. The fool! Left alone, the Corridor is the perfect location for our riffraff to gather and kill one another. And the cost of moving its garbage dumps outside the city walls is a colossal waste of my father's treasure."

She stopped, realizing her digression. "My point is this: Aladdin will not be a problem for us. But his distraction will be his downfall—for now he pays no attention to what I'm about. And when I have the lamp, I will rule with discipline, unlike my softhearted, softheaded husband. Serve me well, Faysal, and I will make you Grand Vizier."

"I will not disappoint you, oh brilliant gemstone of the heavens."

"Then let us begin. Bring the storyteller to me. And if he can't be found in the palace, then try the girl's house. Do you remember the place?"

"Of course, my Princess, how could I forget. One moment I stood in the girl's doorway and the next on the streets of Makkah."

"Then do not rest until Idris is standing on this very spot."

THE LOCK RELEASED WITH EASE, which seemed odd to Aminah. It should have been reluctant with age and disuse. But when the gate glided open on silent hinges, she stood back in alarm. The house was not empty. She quickly closed and locked the gate, then stowed the key and ran.

Aminah ducked into the alley hiding Omar just as the dark figure of a man rounded the nearest street corner. She hid in the shadows as he passed, and then peered after him. To her surprise, he stopped at the back gate, removing the brick and retrieving the key. Only one other person in Al-Kal'as would know its hiding place.

Feeling betrayed somehow, Aminah struggled with the irrational resentment boiling inside her. What was Idris doing in her house? Suddenly she gave in to her anger and bolted from the alley.

He turned anxiously toward the footfalls echoing in the empty street. In the dim light, he didn't recognize Aminah until she was almost upon him. Then his face sagged in disbelief.

"No, you mustn't be here," Idris said, his voice hollow. "I hoped Saladin and Rashid had discouraged you. That you had turned back." Before she could answer, he pulled her through the gate, shutting it behind them, and then rushed down the path that emptied into the courtyard.

Aminah managed to stop him next to the dry basin of her old fountain. "Rashid is back here?" she asked. "We must have been closer to Al-Kal'as than I imagined."

"He arrived today. That's how I knew you might yet come,

but I tell you, Aminah, this is a mistake. You must leave at once."

"But why shouldn't I be here?" she demanded. "You stole my lamp, after all. If you really needed it, why didn't you just ask?" Distraught by fatigue and frustration, she suddenly lashed out at Idris. He caught her arm, and for a moment, as they glared at each other, her faith in him faltered.

Idris shook his head. "I didn't take it for myself, Aminah."

"For whom, then!" she cried. "I find you living in my house, cavorting about Al-Kal'as as Aladdin's royal storyteller, and for all I know, making deals with the Princess."

"You could think this of me?" he asked, his eyes wide with disbelief.

Aminah hung her head. "I don't know what I think."

"I did it for you," he said again.

"Somehow I know that's true, Idris. But you had no right taking the lamp without asking, and so you must remedy this. My heart still believes in you, and that's why I know you'll return the lamp to me. Jinni must have back his home. You don't know what it's done to him to be trapped outside."

"Trapped outside? What are you saying, Aminah?"

Her look was blank. Could it be that he didn't know?

"Are you telling me Jinni isn't in the lamp?" he asked.

"No! I mean, yes! He's out there!" she cried, pointing beyond the wall. "Lying in an alley. He was almost killed, Idris, and I find it difficult not to blame you."

"Jinni's here?" Idris started for the gate. "Help me bring him inside. If he's not in the lamp, then he is without magic."

"Stop!" cried Aminah, following him into the street. "How

do you know he's without his powers? What have you done to him, Idris?"

"I've done nothing—intentionally, that is. Look, I'll explain everything, but first let's get Jinni."

"Did you honestly have no idea he was outside the lamp?"

"No. I swear it. Is Hassan with you?"

Unexpected tears pooled in her eyes. "Because the lamp went missing, Hassan was almost killed. He was too hurt to travel with me."

Idris hung his head. "This plan of mine has gone awry," he said. "How was Hassan injured?"

Aminah drew in a deep breath to steady herself. "I'll share my story, too," she said. "But first, you will tell me every detail of this plan of yours."

"Agreed," said Idris.

As they neared the alley, Aminah put a hand on Idris's sleeve. "Be warned," she said. "Jinni won't appear as you remember."

When they reached Omar, who whimpered as they lifted him to his feet, Idris stiffened—whether at the sight of his battered face or his pig's snout, Aminah wasn't certain. But Idris said nothing as they guided him through the gate and into bed.

"He's in terrible shape," said Idris. "Listen to his breathing. And he's been cursed—but you'll explain that later."

There was an ominous rattle in Omar's chest. *Can a demon, without his magic, die?* Aminah wondered, knowing instantly that she wasn't willing to take the chance. She drew Sixer's ring from her pocket.

"The injuries are even worse for him," Aminah said. "He's not used to pain. I must make this go away."

Idris eyed the ring as she slipped it on her finger. "Magic?" he asked.

"Yes. Perhaps you should leave us."

Idris shook his head.

Aminah turned the ring three times. "Ouch!" she cried, and Idris jumped to her side. "It gets quite hot," she explained as pus-green smoke formed near the foot of the bed.

Idris fell back a step, holding his nose. "The stench! It's unbearable."

Aminah reeled at the smell—Sixer was outdoing himself. The demon's pallid green countenance peeked from the cloud of smoke. "Oh Master," he whined. "Must you summon me? This be an inconvenient time. Yes, very inconvenient."

"Why?" asked Aminah, brushing a hand back and forth in front of her nose. "Are you bathing? In a cesspool?"

Sixer's face, protruding from the cloud, deepened to a dark green. "I be venting!" he cried with such venom that Aminah and Idris flinched. "The curse of the four-digit demon! Foul gases bloat us until we erupt like an angry boil! Oh Master, you be insensitive to summon me now."

Sixer glared at Idris, who was holding his nose and shaking with silent laughter. The jinni's features turned black, and Aminah hurried to apologize. "I didn't know, Sixer. I *am* sorry, believe me."

His color lightened. "I must vent again soon. You want not to be present. Please be quick, Master."

"Yes. It's my other jinni, you see," she said, pointing to the bed. "I am afraid he will die if you don't help him. He's badly hurt."

"Give aid to a two-digit? Even one without magic?" Sixer

stepped from his cloud, shaking his head. Idris seemed shocked at his ragged appearance. "No, no, Master," he said, groveling at her feet. "I cannot."

The worst of the stench had abated, allowing Aminah to hold her ground. "You don't have a choice, Sixer. Besides, you should be ashamed of yourself, giving him a pig's face. You will fix that as a part of his healing."

"That be two wishes, Master. Then your wishes will be gone forever. But no matter, I cannot do this for a two-digit demon."

"It will be done, and it will be done with but one wish. Listen carefully, Sixer—you will not betray me. If you do, I . . . I will cut this ring into a hundred pieces. I will scatter the pieces in a hundred different cities."

Sixer howled, and then lapsed into a coughing fit as he drew in his own stench. Suddenly he began to weep. It was a piteous sound, and Aminah would have covered her ears if she hadn't been using her hands to shield her nose. "Please, gentle Master, please do not destroy the ring. Please do not harm Sixer. I shall do as you request. I always do as my master requests." He threw his arms about her ankles, sobbing in grand fashion.

"Then with honor fulfill *this* request: I wish my jinni—that jinni," she said, pointing, "be healed of all afflictions, including his swine-cursed face." The nearness of Sixer further fouled the air, and her vision blurred under the assault of his noxious gases. "Your ring is safe—if you do exactly as I ask. Heal my jinni, and be gone!"

A new wave of his foul smell washed over them as Sixer snapped his fingers. With a crooked grin, he bowed and disappeared. Idris and Aminah pulled Jinni from the bed and stumbled into the courtyard. Gasping for breath, they fell to the paving stones.

"Where did you come by this onerous beast?" asked Idris. "Or should I say *odorous* beast? Malodorous, to be sure."

"In a thieves' den. I'll explain that later as well. Just so you know, after three wishes, Sixer is finished. I have used two. And he says I can't pass the ring to anyone I know."

"Well, he's certainly not a substitute for your jinni."

"No, but look. He did his job well," said Aminah.

"Who *is* that?" asked Idris, staring at Jinni's unmarred face. "He's too young to be Uncle Omar."

"I really do have a lot to explain," said Aminah. "But as I said, I insist on hearing your tale first."

Idris continued to study Jinni's features. "Yes, his body is repaired," he said, smiling. "But pray to Allah that Sixer's lethal gases haven't addled his wits."

Fourteen

ONCE THE APARTMENT had been aired and Jinni was back in bed, sleeping peacefully, Idris and Aminah escaped to the terrace to sit under the stars.

"I could see the wild desire in your eyes," said Idris as he began to tell his side of the story. "I could see that you would never let me take the lamp—even to save your life."

Aminah clutched herself as if a chill wind were passing, though the night was hot, the air still. "I have grown dependent on magic. I wanted the lamp so badly, I left Hassan when he needed me the most." She looked up, her eyes glistening. "I only desired to help others—was that such a terrible thing?"

"No, of course not."

"I want the lamp," she said, rising from her cushion. "I want it back in my hands now, Idris. Where have you hidden it?"

"Be calm. Don't let this get the better of you. Besides, the lamp isn't here—at least, not right here. It's out in the desert."

Aminah started for the stairs. Idris reached out to grasp her arm. "What are you waiting for?" she demanded. "Take me to it."

"Sit," he said gently. "Hear what I have to tell you. It would be deadly for you to touch the lamp, now that Ashraf has returned to Al-Kal'as."

Aminah pulled her arm away. "Who is this Ashraf? What is his part in all this?"

"That is precisely what you need to hear."

She folded downward, perching on the edge of her silk pillow, and Idris told her how he'd crossed paths with Badr and Saladin in the desert near Makkah. And how he had accompanied her back to Al-Kal'as, winning her attention with his stories and gaining a place in the palace.

"Aladdin took to me right away," said Idris. "He appointed me the Royal Teller of Tales. Quite an honor, but better yet, it kept me in the palace. I could keep a careful watch on Badr and Saladin."

"I was certainly surprised to see Rashid," said Aminah. "Why did he stay in Al-Kal'as after betraying Hassan—particularly when the Princess disappeared to Makkah?"

"Rashid didn't have the opportunity to leave the city. Badr rewarded him with permanent accommodations in the dungeon, and there he rotted until she had need of him again. As it turned out, she believed he was the one with the best chance of finding you."

"But how could that be? He had no idea we were in Tyre."

"Ah, but he'd listened at Hassan's bakery window and heard you speak of two places that seemed important: Aleppo and Tyre. I didn't find out about this until today—Badr kept her secret well."

Aminah held her head in dismay. "It's true. I visited Tyre through Jinni's magic. I swam in the sea for the first time—oh, it was joyous! That's why I chose to move us there. And later I met a dear couple from Aleppo—Talib and Nazreen—when I traveled to Makkah. They were making the hajj, as was I, and they were very kind to me. I thought to visit them one day."

"So you did go to Makkah," Idris said, his tone accusing. "Remember those books about the hajj and the holy city that you had me lug from the bookseller? I had hoped you were planning a trip and would take me along on the pilgrimage. Instead, you went alone by magic."

"That is sand long ago blown over the desert, Idris."

He smiled ruefully. "Yes, and I shouldn't have blown it back to you. Forgive me."

Aminah nodded. "Go on," she said.

"Apparently, Badr chose Aleppo first," Idris continued. "That is where Saladin and the rest were headed when you met them along the road." He paused, rubbing his chin thoughtfully. "On second thought, perhaps it was fortunate that Rashid spotted you, as that sent him back to Al-Kal'as instead of continuing on to Tyre."

"None of this is fortunate," Aminah muttered.

Idris pretended not to hear and continued. "Before Saladin and the others left for Aleppo, something truly curious happened. I was already on my way to Tyre, but I have since discovered that Ashraf insisted on being brought here. I still don't know what he was after, but I am told he seemed pleased afterward."

"Then he found what he was looking for," said Aminah, "though I can't imagine what it could be."

"Perhaps he hoped it would make up for what he lost," Idris said. "Ashraf owned a curious box constructed from a strange substance. I overheard the cleric tell Badr that anything magical loses its power when placed inside the Coffer of Hadim Tebdil—that was his name for the box."

"A box that kills magic," Aminah murmured. "You say he lost it?"

"Yes. He had planned to place the lamp inside the coffer, which would have interrupted any magic associated with Jinni. 'And when I at last bring forth the lamp,' he said to Badr, 'the time will have come to witness the end of your bane. I will annihilate the demon.'"

"But that makes no sense," said Aminah. "Badr desires to control Jinni, not destroy him."

"The Princess needs Ashraf to find the lamp, but she won't let the cleric kill Jinni."

"But how will she stop him?"

"I think Badr has underestimated his power," said Idris. "She may not be able to stay his hand."

Aminah rose and stepped to the edge of the terrace, gazing down on the courtyard. "That box could have been the answer. It would have explained why Jinni lost his magic," she said. "But the coffer went missing, and so . . ." Slowly, Aminah turned to face Idris. "It was you!"

"Yes, I stole the box. I hid it in the desert, burying it deep in the sands. The rock outcropping that once marked the hiding place of your gold ducats served the same purpose for me. Then I paid a soon-to-be-missing guard a handsome sum to embark on a 'secret' mission. He was to retrieve a book of lost stories being held for me in Makkah by a trusted friend, who had acquired it at great peril. I told him the new Sultan had approved this venture, and he was to leave that very moment.

"'Secrecy is vital,' I said to him. 'There are many, perhaps even within this palace, who would kill for this tome. The stories are worth more than a treasure chamber full of gold, and that is why Saladin suggested you—one of his most reliable and trustworthy men—for the task.' I gave him an enormous sum, provided by my enchanted money chest, to pay my friend for the book, to travel in comfort, and to reward his service."

"But there was no friend to be found," said Aminah. "And you were certain he would never return."

Idris nodded. "He left here with enough gold to guarantee it. Besides, who would dare fail Saladin and return to face him? As I hoped, both the Captain of the Guard and the Princess were convinced the poor fellow stole the box."

"I'm beginning to make sense of this," said Aminah. "Or at least, to understand what seemed to make sense to you."

Idris held up his hand. "Let me finish my story before you pass judgment. The mission to find you was still feasible without the box, and so the Princess finally decided to stop chasing after it. She recalled Saladin from the search and commanded him to leave for Aleppo."

"But you were several steps ahead of them."

"Yes. In fact, I returned to Al-Kal'as just as they departed. You should know that Aladdin is your ally. He is the one who helped me get to Tyre. He's also the one who told me Ashraf searched this house."

Aminah shook her head in wonder. "What irony," she said. "As a starving beggar, I went to the Princess for help, expecting a kind heart, when it was Aladdin who would have reached out to me."

"He's reaching out to you now, Aminah. He's been hindering Badr's search as best he can."

"But he is the Sultan," she said. "Couldn't he have stopped her with a wave of his hand?"

"Aladdin is an interloper. Most in the palace remain loyal to the Princess, and he knows this. His handful of faithful men is not enough, but that didn't keep him from trying."

"Someday I must thank him," said Aminah.

"By the way, I should also tell you about Ahab. On my way to Tyre, I stopped in Damascus to visit him," said Idris. "Once the lamp went into Ashraf's coffer, I realized that not only would you become untraceable but also that the good tailor's magic gifts would disappear. I arrived at his door, claiming to be your messenger, and warned him that his powers would be interrupted. I advised him to retire from his craft right away, for who knew if his gifts would ever return. Then I took a day and filled his largest room with gold from my money box."

"Do you think sultans and grand viziers will allow him to say no to their requests?" Aminah asked. "I doubt money alone will remedy his problems, but at least you were thinking of his welfare."

"Considering my plan to help you, it was the best I could do. I also knew Hassan would have to close the bakery, but the loss of his gifts seemed less important."

Aminah decided not to mention Ella, who, without Aminah's gifts, might well be dead by now. "I suppose you planned ahead for yourself," she said. "Put aside a roomful of gold, knowing your money box would soon be useless."

Idris looked uncomfortable. "Yes, I couldn't be without means. At first I had to bury the gold in the desert, along with the box, but now it is here. In my defense, I did the same for you, Aminah."

"True. But I'd rather have kept my lamp."

"If you had, you might be dead. When I reached Tyre, I knew I must hurry," he continued. "Saladin and the others would soon be back on your trail, and Rashid claimed to know where you might be. Though I didn't believe him then, I didn't want to risk it. So during my welcome-home celebration, I spilled sherbet on myself—an excuse to leave. I searched for the lamp and was surprised to find my task easier than expected—I found the same hidden closet with the same combination of symbols to open it. What I thought might take days took only minutes.

"I left the lamp hidden in my room, outside the box, in case Jinni were to sense the immediate depletion of his power. Once all of you had retired for the night, I carried everything to the back gate, loaded the horses, and then slipped the lamp into the box. I rode away hoping no one would notice I was gone until morning. Of course, I thought Jinni was inside the lamp—after all, it's where he claimed to be going when he left the kitchen."

Aminah gazed at him with sad eyes. "Such deceit, Idris. I know you were trying to keep me safe, but . . . And what about Jinni? Didn't you care that you were condemning him to a life trapped in a lamp buried beneath the sand?"

"Believe me, I didn't wish him any harm, and I never planned to leave him buried forever. I knew Badr's patience with Ashraf would eventually wear away, and she'd be done with him. Then I could put the lamp back in your hands.

"Just so you know, my original plan was to have Jinni move your house to another place, but there were two problems with that idea. First, it wouldn't really have helped to move, anyway. If Ashraf got close enough, he'd sense the lamp, no matter where you lived—and he would have traveled relentlessly to find you. And second, if the cleric did locate you, it might be just before a full moon, when you probably wouldn't have wishes left to help you and the others escape. Aminah, I was running out of time, and so I did the one thing I thought would keep Ashraf away: hide the lamp in the coffer."

"But we could have done this together," said Aminah. "Kept the lamp in the box except when we needed it."

Idris shook his head. "And keep Jinni a prisoner? That's what you just accused me of doing. No, you would have found it too difficult."

"He could have lived outside the lamp."

"We realize that now," said Idris, "but who knew how the coffer would affect a jinni not inside his vessel? Besides, I wanted to stay close to Badr so as to react quickly to any turn in her plans. And I wanted the lamp close by—I considered using Jinni against the Princess again, should there be no other alternative."

"Well, what's done is done," Aminah said. "But there is one

more thing I must know: How is it we didn't find you waiting for a caravan in Damascus—or Baghdad?"

"Because I knew that's where you'd look. I thought you'd give up and go home when you saw I wasn't there. How stupid of me."

"So where did you go?"

"I traveled to Jerusalem, and then down to the port of Aylah on the eastern tongue of Bahr Al-Qulzum—the Red Sea. There I boarded a ship and sailed to Al-Daybul, which is not too far south of Al-Kal'as. This route kept me safe from both you and Saladin."

"There is something else I'd like you to tell me," said Aminah. "Why are you in my house?"

"It was gifted to me."

"And when did I do that?"

Idris grinned. "After I returned from Tyre, I thought to wander by your old place and found it empty, though a sign on the main gate said it was now the Sultan's property."

"Badr's doing, I'm sure," Aminah grumbled.

"I don't know why I hadn't visited it earlier," said Idris, "and when I laid eyes on the familiar walls, I knew somehow that I needed to be here. So I asked Aladdin if I might live in it. I offered to pay whatever he required from my wages for the privilege. That's when Badr caught wind of my request and told Aladdin whose house I fancied. I thought all was lost, but to my surprise, she seemed to think it fitting revenge to install a servant of the court in her enemy's home. In truth, she went a step further. 'Gift it to him,' she said to Aladdin, and so he did."

Aminah's eyes flashed, and he was quick to add, "Which really means it's yours again."

She laughed. "That look wasn't for you but rather the Princess. It's just like her to give away something that doesn't belong to her."

"But she thinks everything belongs to her—or ought to," said Idris. "To finish my tale, allow me to say once again that I planned to wait until Badr finally gave up the search for the lamp. Then I'd return it to you. My only other choice, as I saw it, was to kill her, and I'm not much of an assassin."

Aminah smiled. "No, Idris. I can't see you with blood on your hands."

"Now it's your turn," he said. "I would like to hear your story."

Instead of beginning her tale, Aminah pointed to the sky. A full moon hung above the city's towers.

"A wishing moon," said Idris.

"No," Aminah said, her voice melancholy. "A moon without magic."

Fifteen

AS THEY GAZED AT THE MOON, lost in their own thoughts, a dull click disturbed the silent night air. Aminah glanced at Idris, fear in her eyes, and quickly moved to the terrace stairs. "The back gate," she whispered. "Who has the key?"

"I do," said a voice from below.

Aminah stumbled back, colliding with Idris. "It's Aladdin," he said in her ear.

"Come quickly," the young Sultan urged. "The Palace Guard will soon be at the gate."

As they hurried down the stairs, Aminah watched Aladdin's dark figure slip into Idris's quarters. And when she stepped into the lighted apartment, she came face-to-face with him.

Aladdin bowed his head to her. "It is an honor to meet you

at last, Aminah," he said. "I regret we have not the time to visit."

Aminah knelt, reaching for his hand to kiss his fingertips. It was the homage due one of his rank, but Aladdin stopped her. "No," he said. "I plied the lamp to become sultan. In your care, it was much better used. I think the honor is yours." He took her hand, raising her up, and then fell to a knee, touching his lips to her fingertips instead.

Aminah's cheeks flamed. "Thank you," she murmured, "but I don't deserve such praise."

"Nonsense," he said kindly, standing again. "Now, you must be away. Faysal will be here within the hour."

"Who is Faysal?" she asked.

Idris, who had watched in stunned silence, managed to find his voice. "Saladin's replacement," he said. "Aladdin, what led both you and Badr to believe Aminah was here?"

"Rashid saw Aminah on the road to Al-Kal'as, of course, and now Badr suspects she has come to retrieve the lamp from the one who stole it." Aladdin's lips parted in a knowing smile. "And also stole the Coffer of Hadim Tebdil."

Idris rubbed his brow. "I knew no other way to throw Ashraf off the scent but to make the lamp untraceable. I never imagined my plan would be so transparent to everyone, including the Princess."

"At one time or another, all of us have underestimated the beautiful Badr," said Aladdin, his face sagging with sorrow at the thought of her. "However, she only suspects your part in this—she has no real proof—and will have none as long as Faysal finds only the two of us when he arrives."

"Then you must take the horses, Aminah," said Idris. "And

you will need gold." He pulled aside a sandalwood panel and opened an iron door that mirrored the one in Tyre. He reached inside the hidden closet and lifted out a finely tooled leather saddlebag. "I keep this ready for a fast departure. It should be more than enough to get you home without being too much to carry."

"Don't you mean to get *us* home?"

"I can't leave," said Idris. "It would confirm Badr's suspicions."

"He's right," Aladdin said. "If Faysal doesn't find you here, then she'll wonder if Rashid is mistaken about Idris—even though she also knows our storyteller didn't have a mother in Damascus."

Idris groaned. "I'm doubly an idiot. Of course Rashid would know that about me."

"We can tell her I sent you on an errand of secrecy—that we used the story of your mother as a ruse," said Aladdin. "We'll figure out the details after Aminah is gone."

"I'm not leaving without him," she said. "Idris, be sensible—"

He put a finger to Aminah's lips. "I am safe here with Aladdin. Take the gold." As he placed the saddlebag over her arm, their eyes met, and she knew he meant for her to take the lamp as well.

As Idris secured the closet, there was a shuffling noise from the next room, and Aladdin turned toward the sound. Omar stumbled through the doorway. "I am healed!" he cried, plucking happily at his nose. "Why, Aladdin! What a pleasant surprise."

Aladdin drew near, studying Omar's features. "Younger,

certainly," he said softly. "No longer a violet shade, to be sure. Nevertheless, the face is unmistakable. But this cannot be."

"An unfortunate result of applying the coffer's power at just the wrong moment," said Idris. "I'll explain when we have the time. There are traveling robes in the stable. Come—I fear we've talked far too long."

"Aminah, what is happening here?" Omar asked. "Are we leaving Al-Kal'as?"

"Yes," she answered.

"Without the lamp?" He shook his head. "No, I cannot abandon it."

"Don't worry. I'll explain as we go."

Omar turned puzzled eyes on Idris.

"You will have your lamp, Jinni," he said. "But it must stay in the box, Aminah. Do you understand?"

"Of course I understand," she retorted.

Aladdin pushed her from the room, and as they moved toward the moonlit courtyard, she saw him snag a dark leather satchel from the stones outside the door.

"Knowing you might be here—and therefore would be fleeing from Badr—I prepared these provisions so as to hurry your departure," said Aladdin.

Though he'd lowered his voice, it still carried through the darkness, echoing eerily from the deserted buildings. The empty sights and sounds of her old home filled Aminah with an unaccountable, aching loneliness, and she wished more than ever to be back in Tyre with Hassan.

"Again, I am in your debt," she said as Omar took the satchel from Aladdin's hand.

Once in the stable, Idris and Aladdin saddled Idris's two finest stallions. Meanwhile, Aminah and Omar outfitted themselves for their journey from the gear available, such as khuff boots and taylasan robes. Though every item was too large for Aminah, she still managed to clothe herself adequately by the time the mounts were ready.

As they led the stallions from the stable, pounding at the front gate reverberated through the grounds. "Faysal is here," said Aladdin. "Is there another way out?"

"There," said Aminah, pointing.

The back of the estate rested against the city wall, and Aladdin chuckled as he spotted a wooden door set into its blocks of stone. "So that's not a closet for gardening tools, but rather a tunnel leading to the desert," he said. "An unsanctioned exit hollowed out by the former owners, I suppose."

"Probably," said Aminah. "It was here when I bought the place."

The pounding intensified, and Aladdin started toward the gate. "I'll let them in," he called over his shoulder. "Get Aminah out of here, and then come quickly."

"He will say we were grooming the horses while he listened to one of my tales," said Idris.

"An explanation Aladdin has used before, I take it. Fortunate you have four mounts," said Omar. "It leaves two to substantiate your story."

Idris drew open the passageway door to reveal a wooden wall, bare but for a few worn bridles and a dusty cloak. Aminah reached out in surprise to touch it. "Well, this is new," she said.

"It seemed a prudent addition," he answered, pushing the wall inward on creaking hinges.

The passage beyond was barely tall enough for the horses and was sealed at the end with a heavy iron door. As Idris labored to swing it outward, Aminah remembered the stone façade that added to its weight.

"Go swiftly," said Idris, embracing Aminah and slipping a folded piece of parchment into her hand. Before she could ask what it was, the gate was groaning back into position.

When it settled into place, the door blended seamlessly with the city wall's rock face. "It is a mistake to leave Idris behind," Aminah said, staring morosely at the spot where the opening had been. Then she mounted her stallion, and with Omar following, she galloped toward the rock outcropping that marked the lamp's hiding place.

Omar drew even with her. "Where are you leading me?" he called out.

"To rescue your brass dwelling," she shouted against the wind, and Omar beamed.

They skirted the city and came to the outcropping from behind. Leaving the mounts hobbled, Aminah paced off the distance from the rocks to the place where she'd once buried Jinni's ducats. She threw herself down and, in a sudden frenzy, began scooping away soil with her hands. She worked with such intensity that she didn't notice when Omar joined her— until they bumped heads as they flailed in sand.

They sat back, rubbing their foreheads, and laughed with nervous anticipation. "Here," said Omar, "use my shoe for a shovel. I should have thought of it before now."

The excavation proceeded in a more orderly fashion. As the hole deepened, it became too confined for both of them, and so they took turns—one digging while the other cleared sand from the edge. And as they spelled each other, Aminah told Idris's story.

"The Coffer of Hadim Tebdil!" Omar exclaimed when the name came up. "That explains a good deal. Wait, I have struck something solid!"

Aminah could barely contain herself. She wanted to pull him from the hole and uncover the coffer herself. Omar cleared away the last of the sand and then stiffened as he dusted off the coffer's lid. "It is a fell magic," he said in a tight voice, and then climbed from the pit, yielding the box to Aminah.

She eased into the pit and placed flat hands on the coffer's top, as if her touch might divine what lay inside. Though she'd sacrificed so much for this moment, Aminah couldn't bring herself to open the box. Feelings of guilt for abandoning Hassan mingled with fear that the lamp might not be inside. She drew in a deep breath and pried at the lid, which held fast.

After a few tense moments of wrestling with the box, Aminah discovered a latch. When she released it, the top rotated effortlessly to the side on a pivot point. Holding her breath, she knelt over the open container. Within, the lamp lay nestled in a bed of sand. A small leather satchel, overflowing with gold coins, rested against it.

"There's treasure inside! It's mine!" cried the voice of Gindar.

Aminah fell back as he dropped into the hole, shoving her aside. Though there was barely room to move, she threw herself at him.

They clawed at each other, the coffer wedged between them, until Gindar pushed her away with enough force to send her flying from the pit. He scooped up the box and thrust it out onto the desert sand, but before he could follow, Aminah shouted his name. When Gindar turned, she was on him again, launching a fist into his face.

"Oh! Ow!" cried Gindar. He crawled from the hole and lay in the sand, blood coursing through his beard. "Not the nose! Anywhere but the nose!"

Though it was now Omar's voice, Aminah ignored his pain and rushed to the coffer. Without thought to Idris's warning, she lifted out the lamp. As she did, Omar's youthful features softened with age and his nose stopped bleeding. A faint lilac tint seeped into his skin, and Aminah knew she had her jinni back again.

A wild grin stretched around the demon's head, circling twice before snapping back into place. He bellowed with joy, and Aminah leapt back at the sound, laughing. Jinni shot upward, disappearing in a puff of lavender smoke. She guessed where he had gone.

Aminah opened her arms to the moon and tipped back her head. She began to wheel about, spinning faster and faster, the ecstasy of magic filling her body. Moonlight glinted from the lamp, which she held at arm's length until it grew heavy. Finally, she collapsed in the silvery sand and put her ear to the spout. "Are you there?" she asked breathlessly.

"Home again!" Jinni's voice rose from inside.

"But you always hated being trapped in the lamp," Aminah called down to him, laughing.

"Yes, who would have thought I would grow to miss the place. Needs a good cleaning, however."

"Jinni, listen to me," Aminah said, suddenly sober. "We shouldn't have opened the box so soon. Ashraf will have sensed the lamp. He'll know who has it and where we are. Come out, and I'll wish us away."

"Summon me properly," said Jinni. "Give a little rub, for old times' sake."

"Didn't you hear me? We must hurry!" Still, Aminah gave the lamp several brisk strokes with the hem of her robe.

Smoke billowed from the spout, and Jinni made a grand entrance, leaping from the cloud and then exploding into thousands of bright purple fragments. The pieces quickly found one another, reassembling themselves into a somber demon four times the height of a man. Aminah remembered this look from the first time she'd released Jinni from the lamp. He stood bare-chested, a sash the size of a tent girding his waist and an earring like a cartwheel suspended from one lobe.

"Say whatso thou wantest! Thy slave is between thy hands!" Jinni boomed. Then he leaned down, his great mouth with its sharp teeth near Aminah's right ear. "Oh, this is great fun," he whispered.

"I'm very happy for you," Aminah said, unable to suppress a smile. She slipped the lamp into one of her robe's deep pockets, and then sealing the coffer, she wrapped her arms around it. "I wouldn't think of leaving this behind."

"Hold on," said Jinni, shrinking until he was eye to eye with her. "You need not use a wish. Your gift to travel through time and space should have been restored."

"Yes! How stupid of me," she said. "Get back inside the lamp."

Jinni disappeared with a loud bang, and she closed her eyes. Visualizing her courtyard in Tyre, Aminah waited for the icy prickling of her skin. After a full minute, she opened her eyes, and with a wrenching sob, she summoned Jinni.

He popped from the lamp without fanfare. "This is not Tyre," he said.

Aminah looked at him through damp eyes. "I have no power," she whispered.

"Then make a wish. I am quite obviously my old self, so there should be no problem. We will solve this other mystery in a safer climate."

She nodded, picking up the box and slipping the lamp into her robe again. "I wish to be standing in my courtyard in Tyre," she said.

"Done," said Jinni, snapping his fingers and vanishing. But a moment later, his head ballooned from Aminah's pocket. "We are still in Al-Kal'as," he said, looking bewildered.

"Come out," said Aminah, in a voice that nearly failed her. She fished out the lamp and set it on the sand.

Jinni flowed from the spout like thick honey. As he took form, he fell to his knees before Ashraf's box. Then he covered his face and began to wail mournfully, rocking back and forth in the sand until Aminah seized his shoulder.

"What's gone wrong with you?" she cried. "Your skin is lavender. You can grow and shrink and disappear. Where is the rest of your magic?"

"Oh," Jinni moaned, "I fear all is lost. I fear the coffer has forever limited my power. Have you noticed that I cannot even achieve a nice, rich plum color? I am now no more than a cheap magician, and if this is so, then seal the lamp inside that evil receptacle. Bury it again, and I will accept Omar's fate—to fight the influences of Gindar. Oh, I am doomed to a life of bloody noses!"

sixteen

"PERHAPS THE SPELL will lessen in time," said Aminah. "If we are patient . . ."

Jinni shook his head. "That is not the way of things."

"Then all *is* lost," she said, settling onto the ground next to him. She opened the coffer, dropping the lamp inside. Jinni's hint of color faded, and the younger Omar reappeared.

After sealing the coffer, Aminah gave in to her misery. She toppled into the sand, writhing with the agony of facing life without Jinni's magic. She felt so empty, so hollowed out, that it seemed she might simply collapse into nothingness. Against her will, the idea crept into her head that dying was preferable to suffering an obsession for which there was no relief. "I will lie here in the dirt until either Badr finds me or the sun bleaches my bones," she whispered to herself.

But as Aminah teetered on the edge of her existence, Omar reached out and drew her back. He took her hand and stood, pulling her up as he rose. "Forgive me, I spoke in a moment of despair," he said, trying to smile. "There is always hope. Who knows, perhaps you were right about the spell—it may well dissipate in the days to come. We must give this some time to run its course, Aminah, but we cannot stay here."

As she crawled from a place of darkness, Aminah struggled to make sense of Omar's words. "What shall we do?" she asked.

"We must go from here before the Princess follows Ashraf to this place. Let us carry the lamp far from here, sealed in the coffer. As you know, the box eats magic, and so the cleric will not sense its whereabouts or the lamp's as we travel. We will work through this quandary when we have the luxury of time, Aminah. Come!"

A thread of hope was all she needed. Aminah felt renewed life course through her. "But what of Idris?" she asked.

"He has Aladdin," said Omar. "I think he will be safe. Besides, there is nothing we can do for him."

Aminah considered this a moment, and then she said, "You're right, of course. But we can do something for Hassan and Barra—we must get them away from Tyre."

"Yes, that should be our goal," said Omar. "But the Princess will expect us to travel the caravan route. And if we do, it will be difficult to evade her."

"Then we must take a different path," said Aminah.

"You know another way?"

She withdrew Idris's folded sheet of parchment from her robe. "The reason we didn't find Idris in Damascus or Baghdad is that he went south to the port of Aylah and then traveled by sea. As we left him, he pressed this map into my hand. It marks his route."

"Magnificent!" cried Omar. "A shorter land route means fewer bandits. And I do look forward to an ocean voyage. I always thought I should have been one of the sea jinn, housed in a great pink-and-russet seashell. Ah, the feel of salt spray as you face down a sharp gale! The crack and snap of billowing sails! To stand on the deck with Blackbeard the Pirate or Sir Francis Drake!"

"Blackbeard?"

"The future, my dear girl. I speak of seafaring men in the days when ships will travel from one end of the earth to the other! Great ships, each with sails enough to sew a city of desert tents."

"Perhaps you should have lost your memory as well as your magic," said Aminah, and then was quick to add, "I'm only jesting."

"I do hope so," said Omar. "Memories are all that stand between a powerless jinni and madness."

"You haven't lost your sense of drama, either," she said with a smile. "Come on, let's ride."

"No." Omar crossed his arms and grinned.

"No? Why not? Badr will be—"

"There's no need. We have forgotten Sixer!" he cried.

Aminah's lips parted in surprise. "Sixer," she said, almost as if the sound were unfamiliar, and then began to laugh. "Oh, but aren't we simpleminded, Uncle Omar?"

"I trust Idris's mounts will find their way home," he said. "Now, pull out that ring."

Aminah reached into her robe, but her hand came away empty. She looked up, her face pallid. Without a word, she shucked off the robe and searched through every fold. She dug in the pockets of her trousers and shook out her boots. "It was in my pocket!" she wailed. "I made certain before we left Idris."

"Lost in the sand!" Omar cried. "When you struggled with Gindar!"

They rushed to the pit, combing through the grains with their fingers. When the ring didn't surface, they dug deeper, sifting through the sand both in the hollow and in a wide circle around it.

"We can delay no longer," said Omar. He and Aminah lay in the sand, panting. "Or the Princess will have the lamp and our lives."

Aminah nodded, too discouraged to speak, and rose to mount her stallion.

"IDRIS WAS WITH ALADDIN," Faysal told Badr. "The Sultan would not allow me to bring him to you. He was enjoying another of his evenings away from the palace, listening to the storyteller's tales while they curried the boy's stallions."

"Sultan," Badr hissed. "Never again name him so in my presence. He is a lover of street urchins and common thieves. What of the girl?"

"I informed Aladdin that rumor had it she was hiding in her old estate. He seemed alarmed by the prospect and ordered a search. We found no one."

Badr's lips compressed with anger. "You have been deceived!" She stepped closer to her new Captain, lashing out to rake his cheek with her fingernails.

"The lamp is here," said Ashraf.

Everyone turned to the cleric, straining to hear his parched rasping. He was huddled in a corner, peering into a stone amulet that hung from his bony neck.

"And you are just now telling me this?" Badr bared her perfect teeth. "What am I paying you for?" she screamed. "To hide the truth from me?"

Ashraf's cold eyes captured the Princess and held her. It was as if he had opened a festering wound, draining away the corruption, for the venom in her was suddenly gone.

"I detected a surge of magical power," he said, as if nothing untoward had happened. "It came from just outside the city wall, somewhere north of the main gate. It is most certainly the lamp, removed for a brief time from the coffer. I sense the girl is here, as we suspected, but the lamp will not help her escape."

"And why is that?" Badr demanded. "If she has the lamp, why not take herself away with its magic?"

Ashraf frowned, tugging at his beard. "I bound the jinni's enchantments to his lamp. That is why I insisted on searching the girl's estate—to find a strand of hair or a fingernail clipping from the demon's master. A discarded hairbrush provided what I needed. The magic was bound to the lamp's location at the moment I performed the ritual."

"So, the lamp is useless to the girl until she returns to either Tyre or Aleppo—but which of the two?" Badr mused. "We must know, and red-hot steel will reveal it to us." She turned to Faysal, who immediately dropped his hand from his scratched cheek. "Find a way to separate Idris from Aladdin. Then burn the truth from him," she said.

A look of disgust crossed Ashraf's face, but he continued in a voice devoid of emotion. "Even bound, the lamp's power can still be sensed. But the girl has returned it to the coffer, and it is again lost to me."

"Then we can't delay!" Badr cried. "Lead Faysal to the place where you last sensed the lamp. If she's not there, then follow her trail. But hear me, cleric, I want the magic released when you catch her. And I want to be there when you call out the jinni so that I may watch him suffer."

"As you wish," said Ashraf.

Once the cleric and the others were gone, Badr's venomous feelings returned. Though she admitted it had been wise to bind the lamp—otherwise Aminah would have used it to escape Al-Kal'as—she was still furious with Ashraf. Had she not needed the man even more than she needed Faysal, the Princess might have killed him on the spot for keeping the binding charm secret. "The instant he frees the lamp, the cleric will draw his final breath," she said aloud to the empty room.

For the next hour, Badr paced the floors of her apartment, anxiously awaiting word from Faysal. As if expecting to see Aminah fleeing into the desert, she moved back and forth between her rooms and the balcony, where she peered beyond the city wall. But the moon-silvered sands offered her nothing.

When the Captain of the Guard returned, he found the Princess staring at the sky. "Aladdin says the moon governs the jinni's magic," she said, without turning to face him. "Three new wishes granted each time it rounds to its fullest. But I suppose I'll never know for certain if you continue to fail me."

Faysal recognized the quiet danger in Badr's voice. "I have not yet failed you, my Princess," he said carefully. "It is true the girl is gone from Al-Kal'as, but as Ashraf indicated, she has not disappeared by way of magic. Instead, she travels on horseback, and we will run her to ground."

Badr dropped her eyes from the moon. "One more chance, Faysal. But this time, I am coming with you."

AMINAH AND OMAR found the cutoff leading south from the caravan road, but not without searching. They left the trail and guided the horses across the rocky desert toward the rising hills. The map showed the seldom-traveled route leading into the mountains, and they experimented with several narrow ravines until discovering the path.

"Less chance of bandits because there's no one to rob," Aminah said, surveying the rough terrain ahead. Despite the uneven surfaces, the two of them moved faster than a lumbering caravan traveling the well-established roads. Still, it took two weeks to reach the port city of Al-Daybul. The provisions Aladdin had given them barely held out.

When they arrived, Aminah was surprised at how quickly they located a sea captain willing to take them and their horses—and his vessel was casting off the next day. The price of their passage was not cheap, but with the gold Idris had given her, plus the extra they'd found with the lamp, she had plenty to spare.

The voyage across Bahr Al-Hind disappointed Omar. The weather was clear and sunny, and though there was a brisk sea breeze to push the ship along, he was looking to feel the sting of salt spray as he "faced down a sharp gale."

"This Arabian Sea provides a poor sailing experience," he complained, but everyone, especially the sailors, ignored him.

Aminah ignored him as well, busy with her own concerns. She worried about Badr, though she didn't think the Princess could reach Tyre before them. Nevertheless, doubt plagued her, and she knew the only solution to her sleepless nights was to be off ships and horses and to be at home again—only to leave immediately with Hassan and Barra in tow.

From time to time, she was still overwhelmed by a momentary wave of despair about the lamp. However, she was also comforted by the knowledge that Ella at least had Prince Louis and Ahab had gold enough to care for his orphans.

But what of Idris? she asked herself. *And what of Jinni?* Glancing furtively at Omar, she wondered about his future. *If the lamp must remain in the coffer, Gindar will not win out. I'll see to that,* she thought, with a flash of confidence that surprised her.

After two days on the open water, Omar contented himself with standing at the prow, waiting for the occasional burst of seawater to pepper his face. When Aminah joined him, he wouldn't turn from "the teeth of the gale" to look at her—until she said, "You wanted excitement on this voyage, and I think you will have it."

He glanced at the sky, searching for dark storm clouds, but then she pulled him to the stern. "There," she said, pointing to a patch of red on the horizon. "Captain Abdul recognizes the sail. It's a pirate's ship."

SEVENTEEN

OMAR FROWNED at Aminah's news.

"You don't seem pleased," she said, gazing nervously across the gray expanse of water toward the ship. "'To stand on the deck with Blackbeard the Pirate'—weren't those your words?"

"Yes," he grumbled. "But I was only speaking figuratively. I have no desire to actually face the likes of Blackbeard—particularly without my powers." Omar gestured toward the red sail, which seemed nearer now. "Nor do I wish to confront the scoundrel's predecessors."

"Neither do I," said Aminah, her voice hushed. "But the captain doesn't believe he can outrun them."

"The brigands will empty the hold, no doubt," said Omar.

"But worse, they will like as not steal you away from us. Or slit all our throats."

She turned from the sea, covering her face with her hands. "I can't bear it," she cried. "Have I come this far to end like this?"

For the next hour, Aminah kept a terrified eye on the red sailcloth and watched it grow larger. The Coffer of Hadim Tebdil, which was never out of her sight, sat on the deck, held steady between her ankles.

Captain Abdul unfurled every scrap of his own sail and ran with the wind, but the pirate's ship was faster. "Dump the cargo!" shouted his crew, but the captain shook his burly head.

"The blackhearts would catch us still," he bellowed over the wind. "And then kill us for robbing them of their spoils."

The red sail bore down on them until the pirate's vessel skimmed the water but a boat length behind. A man stood at the bow, close enough for Aminah to see the grim smile on his lips—a smile she recognized. Trembling, she reached out to steady herself as the gap closed between the ships.

"Well, hello!" Hammarab called. "I did not think to see you again, my little one. But now that I have, I must know how you escaped the Citadel."

The pirate ship began to pull alongside. At the same instant, Aminah and Omar spotted Iron Toe manning the tiller. He grinned dangerously, thumping his peg leg against the deck.

Omar shuddered. "He means to skewer me with that thing."

"Why are you here and not in the desert?" Aminah cried. They were face-to-face now, only a dozen cubits of salt water separating them.

"I miss the sea!" Hammarab shouted in return. "So Iron Toe and I return for a time every year or two. We both started as pirates, when we were young. Did he tell you he lost that leg rescuing me from a shark?"

As the ships drew even, Hammarab drifted past her, and he called back cheerfully, "I'm pleased to have you back, my dear! Now, Captain, I suggest you furl your sail."

Captain Abdul, seeing words pass between Aminah and the pirate, reached her in several long, sure-footed strides. "You know this man?" he asked angrily. "Have you been playing me the fool?"

"The sail, Captain," called Hammarab as an arrow struck Captain Abdul's helmsman. As the man toppled overboard, the ship veered away from their attackers.

"I was once his captive," Aminah answered. "I watched his army of thieves murder nearly every soul in my caravan. So, yes, Captain, I know Hammarab, and I fear him even more than you do."

The space between the vessels widened, and Iron Toe fought to bring the pirate ship back in line with its prey. Another arrow took the sailor who had stepped in for the helmsman.

"Furl the sail," bellowed Captain Abdul. As his men fell to work, he turned back to Aminah and whispered, "I apologize, Miss. May Allah have mercy on us."

As the captain moved back to the helm, Aminah hoisted the coffer and hurried toward the prow. Panicked, she crouched behind a mound of cargo strapped to the deck, and Omar soon joined her.

"Our fate is sealed," he said, taking her hand. "It has been an honor to serve you, Mistress."

With a hoarse cry, Aminah leapt up. Clutching the coffer, she ran for the hold, weaving from side to side with the rocking of the ship.

"Where are you going?" Omar shouted. "You cannot hide."

She had taken only a few steps when the two ships butted against each other. The deck tilted beneath her, and Aminah crashed headlong onto the sopping planks. The box flew from her grasp as she threw out her arms to break her fall.

When Omar reached her, the ship had steadied. The sail was coming down, and the vessel began losing speed. Iron Toe again closed the distance between them.

Dazed, Aminah was slow to realize the coffer lay open, its contents strewn across the deck. Omar, his face now tinted purple, helped her stand, and they hurried to scoop up the lamp before it rolled away from them. The sand that had been its bed inside the box lay glued to the wet planks.

Aminah held the lamp to her breast, and crawling back to the coffer, she dropped it in and swiveled shut the lid. When she turned to find Omar, he was kneeling beside her, a sand-covered trinket in his cupped hands.

"The ring," he whispered. "It must have fallen into the coffer as you scuffled with Gindar—and been covered by sand."

Unable to fathom this sudden turn of fate, Aminah plucked up Sixer's ring without a word. She left the coffer in Omar's care and again slid out of sight behind the mound of cargo. A moment later, the demon's putrid green vapors enshrouded her.

"Last wish! Last wish," crowed Sixer, even before his skeletal form appeared. His voice was all but lost amid the triumphant din rising from the pirate ship.

"Yes," said Aminah, taking a reluctant step closer to be certain Sixer could hear. "You'll soon be free of me."

"Oh, joy! Ask away, Mistress. Ask away!" The demon danced in circles.

Hammarab's voice rose above the mayhem. "Captain," he shouted as grappling hooks flew over the gunnels. "Send over the girl, and at least her life will not be forfeit. As for the rest of you . . ."

The ships moved together as pirates heaved on ropes attached to the grappling hooks. Aminah peered around the crates to see Hammarab perched on the gunnel, ready to jump aboard. He and his men had scimitars drawn.

"Rid us of these pirates," she cried to Sixer.

The jinni floated upward until he could see over the cargo. At the sight of Hammarab's crew, a malevolent grin cleaved in half his mottled face. He chortled with wicked glee. "Oh, but this be a pleasure!" he said, snapping his fingers. "Your wish be granted."

Instead of disappearing, the demon hovered in place. A great cry arose as Aminah pocketed the ring. Then she stepped from behind the crates in time to see the pirate ship shudder. The thief lord fell back as the boat folded in on itself with the shriek of planks pulled asunder.

"What are you doing?" Aminah screamed, but Sixer ignored her, his eyes riveted on the splintering vessel.

The pirates screamed, scrambling to throw themselves into the water, but each brigand struck an invisible barrier and was thrown back to the deck. With a deep groan, prow and stern met in the air, and the ship split in two. Water engulfed the shattered hulk as the mast toppled, and the ship slipped beneath the waves. Horrified but unable to look away, Aminah watched Hammarab struggling to swim free, but without so much as a sound, he was sucked into the abyss. In an instant the ship was gone, the sea swallowing the pirates' cries.

An eerie silence followed. "The Delhán! Sea demon!" one of the sailors gasped, disturbing the stillness that had settled over the crew. Certain the same fate would take them, Abdul's men fell to the deck in fear.

Aminah turned to the sound of a satisfied sigh. Sixer still lingered to witness the aftermath of his dark magic, but then, with the same gruesome grin aimed in her direction, he vented.

The sailors shrieked and leapt to their feet at the roar of Sixer's explosion. Every eye followed as the force propelled the demon forward. He caught his toes on the edge of a crate, sending him spinning above the crew, and as he passed over, the trailing stench forced the men back to the deck.

The tumbling green creature erupted into flame, confirming the sailors' fear of sea demons. The men would have shrieked again, but the jinni's gas left them choking and gasping for air. Sixer landed in the sea with a sizzling splash and disappeared.

"How was this possible?" Aminah asked, glancing at Omar. Then she turned toward the spot where Hammarab's vessel had been swallowed by the waves.

"I assume you refer to the rule that jinn may not kill," Omar answered, his eyes surveying the calm surface. "But they may sink a ship. What happens afterward . . . well, that's up to the sea."

Aminah was stunned by the unexpected destruction of the pirates' ship. For some reason, she'd imagined that Sixer would transport the vessel a hundred, perhaps a thousand leagues away. Overcome by the savagery, she felt her knees buckle, and she crumpled to the deck.

While Omar tended to her, Captain Abdul revived the crew with a tongue-lashing. "Up, you fear-crazed louts!" he bellowed. "What are you waiting for? More pirates? Another demon? Throw off the grappling hooks! Hoist the sail!"

Only after the ship was safely under way did the sailors turn on Aminah. "Salim saw the girl consorting with that monster!" cried one of them. "Tell the captain, Salim."

The oldest of the men was pushed forward. "Yes, indeed," he said. "I was tightening down the crates at the bow when I saw."

"You were hiding behind them, more like," grunted Abdul, and the crew barked with tentative laughter.

"Yes, well, I was there to see this girl"—he pointed with a bony finger—"call the Delhán from the sea."

"He did not come from the sea," said Omar, and all eyes fastened on him. "I mean . . ."

"He means that the creature suddenly appeared on deck," Aminah said, rising up on shaky legs. "Surely you don't think I had anything to do with that?"

"She talked to him as if he was her slave," Salim insisted. "'Ask away, Mistress,' it said to her. I swear it!"

"And did she?" asked Abdul.

Salim looked confused.

"Did she ask anything of the creature!" shouted the captain.

"Yes," the old sailor answered. "'Rid us of these pirates'— those were her exact words. I swear it."

Abdul froze Aminah with his fierce, dark eyes. His bushy

brows furrowed above them like storm clouds. "I believed you about the pirate," he rumbled. "What of these charges?"

Still captured by his gaze, she decided to give him some of the truth. "It was a jinni," Aminah said. The crew moaned again, and as one body, they took a step back.

"He appeared, wanting revenge on the pirate," she continued. Aminah sensed Abdul was a good man and so felt a tinge of guilt at her lie. "I didn't ask why there was bad blood between them, but he said he would gladly save us if I'd but ask. It seems a jinni cannot act on his own but must be commanded. I dared not deny him—and you should be glad about that!"

The crew huddled closer together, gaping at her in silent disbelief. At last, a voice from their midst called out. "Throw her overboard!"

"Overboard with her!" chorused the knot of men.

"Perhaps she is herself a jinneeyeh—a demon of the female breed," suggested Salim. "If we drive her off, then we must strew the deck with salt to keep her at bay."

The men howled and surged forward. As if a single being, they tossed Omar aside and lifted Aminah in a fluid motion. She screamed as the mob-creature began to rock, building the momentum to fling her far into the sea.

"Stop!" roared Abdul. "I give the commands on this ship, and I don't recall ordering you to dispose of anyone. Put the girl down."

The men hesitated, and then began to tip Aminah downward—but in the direction of the water.

"On the deck, you nimwits!" The captain cuffed the nearest sailor and turned his hand to another. The mob lowered Aminah to the planks. Then it separated into individual men, who each shuffled toward the center of the ship.

"You are but a pack of superstitious children," said Abdul. "If Aminah consorted with a jinni to save your worthless skins, then she's right—you ought to be grateful."

A handful of salt landed on the deck, scattering across the planks and sprinkling Aminah's feet. "Who did that?" Abdul demanded.

When no one answered, he threw up his hands. "I ought to flog the lot of you. And I will, if I hear another word about a jinneeyeh or throwing anyone overboard. Now clean up this salt and get back to work!"

The captain turned to Aminah. "Don't thank me," he said as she opened her mouth. "My men have a point—you are a suspicious one. But if you can sink a pirate ship with your magic, I ask myself what else you might do. Therefore, I prefer to forget the matter and get you to shore with all haste."

"You'll not put us off at the first port, will you?" asked Aminah.

The captain cast a troubled gaze across the water. "No," he answered. "I will honor our contract. But may Allah bless us with a brisk wind and a safe sea. I want you off my ship."

It was a subdued Abdul who piloted his vessel in the days that followed. His men were still unsettled, constantly scanning the water for danger. They moved silently in response to his curt orders, and Aminah and Omar made an effort to stay out of their way. And they avoided her. But once, when she awoke in the morning, a line of salt encircled her. She swept it up without telling the captain.

When the ship finally approached the southern coast of the

Arabian Peninsula, everyone's spirits lightened. They landed at several ports, including Al-Shihr and Adan, and though the captain was speaking to her again, Aminah chafed at the days spent loading and unloading cargo. It seemed forever until the ship rounded the bottom of the peninsula and entered Bahr Al-Qulzum, sailing northward to Aylah.

To Omar's delight, storms plagued the rest of their voyage. He stood braving every gale and licking the salt spray from his lips, while Aminah curled up out of the elements and nursed a queasy stomach.

The stiff headwinds had slowed their progress, sometimes bringing them to a standstill, but on their last day at sea, the storms abated. The sky was as clear and bright as a sapphire, and that evening a brilliant sunset welcomed them to their final destination. In the red glow, Aminah dragged Omar to the hold to prepare the horses. The animals were saddled and loaded a half hour before the vessel docked at Aylah, and so she shifted from foot to foot, unable to bear the ship's leisurely drifting.

At last, she and Omar led their mounts onto the quay, and the crew all but cheered to have them gone. As they moved beyond the bustle of sailors unloading the hold, Aminah could barely contain her excitement. She wished it were earlier so they might start for Jerusalem without delay.

"Let's find a khan," she said, stopping to further secure the baggage strapped behind her saddle. "Ships and sleep don't mix—especially when one might awake to find herself sleeping with the fish. I need a good night's rest before starting our long ride. Don't you agree?"

Though Omar had pulled up to wait for her a short distance

away, near several towering stacks of cargo, Aminah thought it odd that he didn't answer. She turned to find his mount standing alone.

A sense of foreboding kept her from calling out to him. The guttering torchlight, struggling to illuminate the quay, dimmed her vision, and so she crept forward for a better look. Omar's horse whickered, throwing back its head, and a dark figure stumbled from behind the wall of crates. Even before the flickering light caught his face, Aminah knew it was Omar. The blade of a scimitar settled against his throat as another figure stepped into view.

"Rashid," Aminah breathed. She turned to run back to Abdul, though she knew he wouldn't be pleased to see her. Several Palace Guards materialized, blocking her retreat.

Facing Rashid and Omar, she saw Ashraf appear. The Princess Badr, flanked by her guards, followed. It was as if a cold band of iron tightened around Aminah's chest.

"Shocked to see me?" the Princess asked amiably. Then her voice hardened. "I have yet other surprises for you."

A guard dragged Idris forward. His hands were tied, and he seemed barely conscious as he collapsed on the ground before Aminah. Then Aladdin, gagged and bound, was flung in the dirt beside him.

eighteen

THE PRINCESS COMMANDED her men to take the prisoners beyond Aylah's outskirts. By a stagnant pool under a few stunted palm trees, the procession stopped. A campfire lit the empty surroundings. It was a place where Badr could conduct her business in private.

"Like Aladdin, weakness has always been your undoing," Badr said as Aminah and the others were thrown to the sand at her feet. Her small mouth puckered with disdain. "You are too soft inside. . . ." She hesitated, unable to make herself speak Aminah's name.

"Soft?" Aminah asked, meeting Badr's steely gaze. "I care about other people, if that's what you mean. If so, then I am indeed soft and proud to say you're right." She glanced at

Aladdin as one of the guards pulled him toward a palm tree, and then continued. "But even one as hard as you, Princess, should fear a sultan's wrath."

Badr followed Aminah's eyes to her husband, who was being lashed to the tree trunk. She laughed and said, "Aladdin is no sultan. He is street filth like you—and a traitor to me. And though he commands an army of beggars in Al-Kal'as, he sadly has few stalwarts in the palace. It was an easy matter to spirit him away from the city—and your storyteller, as well.

"And as you will see, poor Idris was . . . persuaded, shall we say? Yes, persuaded to tell me about Tyre and his own route back to Al-Kal'as from there. Faysal, reveal to her his pain."

The Captain of the Guard dragged Idris forward. Faysal then ripped away his shirt, and Aminah gasped. Angry scars laced his bare chest, some of the burns still crusted and weeping. Tears tumbled down Aminah's face, but Idris did not raise his head to see them. "Forgive me," he murmured.

"Such is what happens to the men in this girl's life," Badr said to Omar, a pleasant smile on her lips. "I don't know where she found you, but I'd think twice about remaining in her company."

"Yes, good advice," said Omar, backing toward the horses. "Good-bye, Aminah. It has been a pleasure, my dear Princess. Nice to see you again, Idris, but I must be off." He was halfway into his saddle before Faysal pulled him back to the ground.

"Where *did* you find this simpleton?" Badr asked, neither expecting nor waiting for an answer. "Faysal, fetch the coffer."

The Captain of the Guard lifted Ashraf's box from Aminah's gear and held it out to the Princess. "I have suffered much to achieve this moment," she said. "Ashraf, bring out the lamp."

The cleric took the container and swiveled the lid aside. With care, he set the coffer on the sand and drew out the lamp. At the sight of it, Badr placed a hand on Faysal's arm to steady herself.

"Give it to me," she said in a small, trembling voice.

Ashraf handed her the lamp, and Badr held it like a long-lost child. Aminah was stunned at the unaccustomed gentleness both in her touch and in her eyes. But the oddly tender moment passed. "Faysal," Badr said, her voice once again like flint, "we do not need excess baggage on the return trip. Before Ashraf performs the unbinding ritual, dispose of it in the desert."

With a toss of his head, Faysal motioned to his men, who moved toward the prisoners. No one but Aminah had noticed the difference in Omar, whose features and complexion had subtly altered when the lamp was freed from Ashraf's box. She wondered fleetingly if there was now enough demon in Omar to survive the guards' scimitars.

"Leave Aladdin," Badr said to her Captain of the Guard. "He needs to witness his dear wife's rise to power. Then I'll decide his fate. However, take that one." She nodded toward Rashid.

Rashid stood between Ashraf and the Princess. His disbelieving eyes flicked from one to the other. As Faysal started toward him, Rashid reached into his jubba and, spitting at Badr's feet, drew forth a dagger.

The Captain of the Guard cried out, and the Princess leapt back. But Rashid fell on Ashraf, burying the knife to its hilt in the cleric's breast. A moment too late, an arrow from Faysal's bow pierced Rashid's heart.

Screaming, Badr fell to her knees beside Ashraf and lifted

his head. She begged him to unbind the lamp, but the light faded from his eyes. The Princess went limp, dropping the dead man's skull into the sand.

Aminah thought she recognized the look on Badr's face. She must have worn the same expression when she and Jinni discovered the lamp was useless. It was the face of defeat—of loss, final and complete. But to her surprise, Aminah realized it was worse for the Princess. She was left without any purpose for existence because she had no one other than herself. Her faith had resided in the lamp alone.

Quiet settled over the oasis. No one moved, except Badr, who crawled over to the fallen lamp. "Surely the cleric's death released the spell," she said to herself. Taking up the lamp, she rubbed it with increasingly violent strokes. When no jinni appeared, she cried out in anguish, but continued working the brass surface until her skin cracked and bled.

At last, Faysal laid a restraining hand across her fingers. "It is useless," she murmured.

"Shall we kill the others?" Faysal asked, as if to distract the Princess from her misery.

For an instant, the old heat smoldered in Badr's eyes, but Aminah spoke out, not giving her a chance to answer.

"Let us go, Princess," she said. "Let us go, and I will give you this." She reached into her pocket and brought out Sixer's ring. "The power of a jinni resides within it."

Badr nodded to Faysal, who plucked the ring from Aminah's grasp. He gave it over to the Princess, who examined it with care.

"A jinni ring, you say." The Princess polished it with the hem of her robe, then set it on her open palm. The wild hope in her eyes faded as the moments passed, and she closed her fist on the ring. "You think me witless? Did you imagine I'd release you with thanks before trying it?"

"Listen to me," said Aminah, but Badr raised her face to the stars and howled. It was a feral sound, laden with fury and fear, and it chilled every heart.

The horses whinnied and pulled at their traces as the Princess threw down the ring and scooped up the lamp. "We come full circle," she hissed. With lightning speed, Badr hurled the lamp at Aminah's face.

For an instant, Aminah became the beggar girl again, standing below Badr's balcony. But in the next instant, she leapt back, and the lamp collided with her chest this time, rather than her forehead. Still, it struck with enough force to take her down, where she lay gasping for breath.

"That is not the way of things," she wheezed. "Slip it on your finger, and I will show you what to do."

Panting with emotion, Badr squatted in the dirt to retrieve the ring. "Show me or die this instant."

"Or show you and die anyway?" Aminah asked. "No, Badr, it is time to bargain. Set us on our mounts. Aladdin, too—you have no need of him. Stack the bows and quivers beyond the firelight. We will ride to the edge of the oasis, and I shall call out the directions. I will not move until the jinni appears. You have my word."

"And why should I not simply burn the truth from you?"

"Perhaps you could. Perhaps not. If I have lied to you, Faysal can run us to ground with little effort."

"And if you are telling the truth, what would keep me from commanding the jinni to bring you back?"

"Nothing, I suppose," said Aminah, her voice tinged with defeat. She had hoped to hold from Badr the truth about Sixer, but now she had no choice. "Nothing but the waste of a precious wish, that is. This jinni will only give you three."

"At each full moon?" Badr asked, puzzled.

"No, just three, and then you are done. But that is better than no wishes at all, and with them, you can become sultan. To waste a wish tracking down a beggar girl seems silly, don't you think? Take my offer. Give us a fighting chance, Princess."

Badr shrugged, unable to muster the energy for torture, and nodded to Faysal. He in turn signaled his men, and two of them collected the bows and quivers and carried them into the night. Two others brought forth the horses.

Faysal cut Aladdin free, who pulled the gag from his mouth and hurried to Aminah's side. "Thank you," he said with a sad smile.

Once mounted, they walked their horses toward the open desert, stopping at a point where they could see Badr in the firelight but she could not see them. Because the Princess was an enemy rather than a friend, Aminah prayed that Sixer would accept her as his new master. Drawing in a nervous breath, she called out to Badr. "Turn the ring around your finger three complete revolutions. The jinni will appear."

As Badr rotated the ring, she shrieked at its searing heat, but her cries of pain suddenly turned to delight. Sixer's putrid green smoke formed a halo around the fire pit.

"Oh mighty master," Sixer whined, his voice penetrating the darkness where the riders waited. "I be not well, not well at all. Nevertheless, I be the slave in thy grasp. Ask of me, and I shall obey."

Aminah waited no longer. "Let's ride," she said.

They galloped into the night with an ear turned to the mud hole behind them. There was no sound of pursuit.

Look what we accomplished, Aminah thought as the firelight disappeared from sight. *And mostly without magic.*

She patted the folds of her robe, touching the lamp's bulge. It was still Jinni's home—she couldn't have left it behind. *I'll keep it as a remembrance of better times,* she told herself.

Then her mind turned to Hassan. "And a reminder that the best times lie ahead," she whispered.

IN TEN DAYS, they approached Tyre. But as the four riders paused on a rocky stretch of beach, gazing up at her estate, Aminah was already calculating how quickly they could gather their belongings and be off again. Though she believed the Princess wasn't likely to use a wish against her, she didn't discount Badr's keen thirst for revenge. She might still decide to send Faysal after her.

Despite her impatience to leave again, Aminah's heart leapt at the scene spread out before her—the house, the sea, and the city in the distance. "We're home," she said, with a sigh.

"And it seems home agrees with Omar," said Idris.

Aminah turned to her jinni. As they'd traveled northward, a light purple tint had continued ebbing and flowing through his face, but now he possessed the look of an overripe grape.

"Your skin!" she cried.

Jinni stared at the deep color in his hands, and then he sprang from his horse, feeling his face as though dark purple were palpable. With a joyous roar, he sent his head spinning on his shoulders, jets of violet steam spewing from his ears. "I am I again!"

He stood still, eyes closed, and breathed in the sea breeze that combed through the coarse grasses. "How is it I did not notice sooner?" he asked, and then looked toward his friends. "Full power courses through my limbs."

"Is the lamp unbound?" Aminah asked, her heart leaping. She dismounted to retrieve it from her saddlebags. "And if so, why now?"

Jinni, in the midst of a mighty backflip that took him high above Aminah's head, paused in midair at her question. He swooped down to land before her and said, "I believe I understand now. Ashraf bound the lamp to its location at the time of the binding ritual—which, of course, was here. If that is true, my magic works only in this tiny part of the world."

Aminah stopped plucking at the leather straps sealing the saddlebag. "But we *can't* stay here! Badr knows we're in Tyre. Eventually, she'll send Faysal to finish with us."

"But she also believes the lamp has lost its power," said Aladdin. "Perhaps she won't find chasing after you worth the effort any longer."

"No," she said. "The Princess's head has cleared now, and she realizes it was a mistake to discard the lamp. Badr knows its magic is bound to Tyre, and from here, she could wield its power. Besides, she still has a score to settle with me."

"It matters not whether the Full Moon of Full Moons follows us," said Jinni, "for I am the slave between thy hands, oh kind Mistress, and with but one wish—no, make that two—your fears shall be set aside."

"And what wishes would those be, oh demon of the lamp?"

she asked with a wistful smile. "I'm reluctant to return to my old ways of plying your magic without so much as a thought. I simply want an unfettered life with Hassan—and now here he is, almost in my arms! Still, what do you have in mind?"

"All in good time," said Jinni. "But first, let us indulge in Barra's superlative cookery!"

nineteen

IN THE VELVETY DUSK of a future time, two figures shimmered into view at the entrance of a stable in northern France. Surreptitiously, they eased open the heavy wooden doors and were greeted by the sweet scent of fresh-cut hay—and the gentle whickering of horses hidden in the dark. At the sound of snapping fingers, a strange golden light flickered and blossomed in midair to illuminate the interior.

"I see the stable boy did his job," said Jinni. A magnificent carriage stood waiting with its horses already in their traces.

"Shall we be off to the Royal Masked Ball?" asked Aminah. Though she tried to sound jovial, her voice was weak, and she leaned against the door, suffering from the inevitable nausea that accompanied time travel.

Ignoring her discomfort, Jinni grinned. "Am I to handle the coach again?"

"Of course," she answered. "Just give me a little time to recover and then rearrange myself. I retched in Ella's room the first time I visited, you know. She was very impressed."

Jinni laughed and attended to the horses while Aminah closed her eyes and waited for her stomach to settle. The moment she felt better, her magical thawb began to rustle, reforming itself as well as its occupant. Soon Aminah was encased in a blue-green gown befitting a fairy godmother, with a rounded face and coiffure to match.

"Now, ready yourself," she said.

The demon pivoted in a circle, and when he faced Aminah again, a tall, light-complexioned fellow in a powdered wig and feathered hat stood gazing at her. "The perfect footman," she said, glancing at his tight breeches and his jacket festooned with gold braid.

Jinni sighed with pleasure. "Oh, this is great fun," he said as his figure began to swell.

"Wait! Can you grant wishes as a footman?" she asked.

The footman cast a look of such disdain that it was Aminah's turn to laugh. "Something more for Ella?" he asked.

"I'm reluctant to use a lot of magic, but what I started with Ella must be finished. She needs one more gift: the gift of invulnerability."

"You wish her to live forever?" asked Jinni.

"No, but I want her protected from harm until her normal life span is ended. She will be living in dangerous circumstances—a commoner who will one day rule as queen. She'll have many enemies."

Jinni snapped his fingers. "So be it."

Aminah nodded, happy to have Ella's protection in place, and then watched with interest as the footman began once again to swell. She covered her ears when he'd inflated to the point of bursting, and a moment later he exploded with the roar of a cannon. A haze the color of mulberries darkened the stable, and when it cleared, there were three of him, though none looked alike. "The footmen and coachman at your service," the threesome chirped in perfect unison.

Aminah clapped her hands. "You're a marvel, Jinni!"

The two footmen—one tall and gaunt, the other short and round—swept off their feathered caps and bowed to her. She giggled as they helped her into the carriage. Then they took their positions outside, standing on a platform at the back.

The coachman, whose swarthy complexion hinted of purple, stopped at the carriage window. "Ella is staying with the miller's daughter, as I recall."

Aminah nodded.

The driver leapt nimbly to his seat, taking up the reins. Six lily-white horses pawed the ground, anxious to stretch their legs. "Hi-yo, Silver—away!" he cried, and then leaned over the side to say, "I borrowed that from American television."

She hadn't the faintest inkling what he meant. But before she could ask, her head snapped back against the seat as the carriage catapulted from the stable.

"Slow down!" The wind threatened to steal Aminah's voice. "People will notice!" The horses' hooves skimmed above the ground, and the carriage flew down the roadway with the speed of an arrow.

"I do love a fast horse," cried the coachman, without turning to look inside the carriage.

"As do I," called one of the footmen.

"Yes, indeed," said the other.

Aminah rolled her eyes as the coachman reined in the horses.

"You had best sit back and practice your French," the driver said.

"Yes, Mother," she replied, and the three demon servants laughed.

Aminah leaned back into the soft seat cushions. Her French was quite good enough, as Jinni well knew. She had long ago come to realize that language would be a troublesome barrier to her work, and so she'd used a wish to remedy the problem. Now she understood and spoke any tongue, as the need arose, though she was never quite sure how the gift worked. Did she truly speak French or did Ella, for instance, simply hear French?

Before long, Aminah heard a chorus of frogs croaking its serenade, and then the coach drew up to the mill. The great water wheel was locked in place for the night, and candlelight streamed from the adjoining cottage windows.

At the sound of carriage wheels, the cottage door opened, and Ella stood silhouetted against the light. Aminah saw the miller's wife hug the girl, and this simple gesture brought a lump to her throat.

As the door eased shut and the girl approached them, Aminah stepped from the carriage. "Are you ready for this night, my dear?" she asked, amazed as always at the matronly pitch of her voice.

"I'm a bit frightened," said Ella, who was dressed in an exquisite new gown Aminah had left for her at the cottage, "but I am quite prepared."

Ella was bathed, coiffed, perfumed, and, indeed, quite ready for the ball. In fact, illuminated by the carriage lanterns, she seemed more dazzling than ever. *Prince Louis hasn't a chance!* Aminah thought smugly.

"Now you know precisely what you must do tonight?" Aminah asked, hugging the girl. "And in the days to follow?"

"Yes," Ella answered. "Should I tell you?"

Aminah laughed, a seasoned sound that matched her stocky figure and wrinkled face. "No, that's not necessary," she said, pushing aside a strand of gray-white hair (also part of the thawb's artful illusion).

The footmen helped Ella into the carriage. Then Aminah had the taller of the two set an enameled box laden with gold— French coins rather than dinars—on the miller's doorstep.

"The roads are dark, driver," Aminah called. "Let's fly! Brace yourself, Ella."

With an undignified whoop, the coachman cracked his whip. The carriage spurted forward with blinding speed, which Ella took in perfect stride.

They slowed as they left the country and approached the congested streets of the city. Near the palace, Aminah called for the driver to stop. "This is where I leave you, my dear," she said, kissing Ella's cheek.

"You seem dressed for the occasion," said Ella. "Will I see you inside?"

"You will not see me, my dear, but I will be watching," Aminah answered as she secured the girl's mask in place. Its glorious peacock feathers arched from Ella's face like out-stretched wings. "The prince is yours," she said, stepping from the coach.

As the carriage left her, Aminah melted into the shadows of an alleyway. Her thawb again rearranged her appearance. Now she stood taller, with dark tresses and a face that was thirty years younger and distinctly French. It was the way guests at the ball would expect another guest to look. She was festooned in a lemon-yellow party gown, wide and floor-length, with long, puffed sleeves. The thawb, which managed every detail, had also topped her head with the appropriate curls and combs.

When the carriage returned for her, the coachman whistled at the sight of his passenger. "It's what French ladies wear to such occasions," Aminah said tartly.

As they approached the palace, she donned a mask that represented the flaming rays of the sun, and soon Aminah, as fortune would have it, was following Sophronia, Marie, and their mother up the stairs and into the ballroom. Marie gazed about the opulent hall, eyes wide at the sight of cascading streams of wine and tables laden with delicacies. But her sister wore a dark scowl.

As was the fashion, a third skirt encircled Sophronia's waist and lay open at the front. Aminah noticed that the girl's hand repeatedly wandered beneath the skirt's heavy folds.

Though bothered by Sophronia's odd behavior, Aminah turned her attention to Ella. Most of the guests had also turned their attention to the mysterious girl and her prince. Louis held her tightly in his arms as they moved across the floor, and he always seemed unhappy when a particular dance required partners to rotate.

Though she was asked, Aminah declined every offer to join the lighthearted throng on the ballroom floor. Through the rest of the evening she kept Ella in sight and was overjoyed to see that the prince kept her by his side every moment.

As midnight approached, Aminah worked her way closer to Ella. At the same time, on the opposite side of the ballroom, Sophronia pushed Marie aside and disappeared into the crowd. It was too late when Aminah spotted her.

Sophronia's face, uncovered now, was its own mask—a mask of pitiable jealousy. Ella was laughing at something the prince had just whispered in her ear when her stepsister struck. From her third skirt she pulled a small, desiccated pig bladder—thin and swollen with its contents—and drew back her arm. There was a scream, and someone struck her elbow. The bladder arched upward, coming down on Sophronia's head and bursting open. Aqueous pig manure drenched her hair and shoulders and drained down the front of her dress.

The crowd stepped back, both at the stench and at Sophronia's unearthly wail. Everyone's attention was riveted on the disgusting scene as two Palace Guards, their noses wrinkling at the odor, dragged the shrieking girl from the hall. Even Prince Louis moved closer to get a better look.

Then another scream ripped through the ballroom, and every eye turned to the sound. Some were quick enough to see the point of a narrow dagger plunged into Ella's throat.

The attacker, draped in dark party clothes and a grinning mask, bolted for the door, but several gentlemen in their finery laid hold of him. "A hired assassin, from the look of things," one of them called out, and several ladies fainted.

The prince knelt over Ella, who had dropped to her knees,

clutching her throat. Aminah stood back, smiling behind her mask. Gently, Louis pulled her hands aside, and the knot of people around them drew in a single, mighty breath.

No blood—not even a scratch. Now Aminah pushed through the crowd and also knelt by Ella. "The knife glanced from her locket," she announced, and the crowd released a collective sigh.

The prince raised Ella to her feet and kissed her hand. The throng cheered as he reached out to lift her mask, but she stayed his hand as the clock in the palace tower began to chime midnight. "Oh, I must go!" she cried, breaking free and running for the stairs.

In shock, Louis stared after Ella, unable to give chase as the revelers closed in behind her. By the time he fought his way to the stairs, the girl was gone. He started down the steps, ordering everyone to stay behind.

He longed to call out her name, but he didn't know it. Ella had deigned to say it, which at the time Louis had found charming. Now he cursed himself for not insisting she tell him.

When he came to the bottom of the staircase, he stopped short. A glass slipper lay on the last step, glinting in the moonlight. He knelt to pick it up.

"It belongs to your love," a voice behind him whispered. He turned to find the woman dressed in yellow—the one who'd knelt by the girl and determined a locket had saved her life.

"And how do you know this?" Louis demanded. "If you know her, then you must tell me who she is—where I can find her."

"I can only tell you this," the woman said. "If you truly

love this girl, then you are meant to find her. That slipper is your key."

"You speak in riddles!" Louis started up the stairs toward her. "Please, tell me what this means."

The woman smiled at him and vanished.

twenty

"NOW THAT WE HAVE Sparrow with us, I believe I'm done with magic," said Aminah. "At least for the most part."

The Alliance of the Lamp lounged on the terrace, faces lifted to the cool sea breezes. The moon would be full by week's end, and they sat in its soft light, the remnants of a sumptuous meal scattered around them.

"Then you have ended on a sweet note," Barra said. She drew Sparrow close, kissing her on both cheeks. The moment they laid eyes on each other, the two Barras had become inseparable.

"But Aminah, are you sure?" said Sparrow, pulling away from Barra to hop from foot to foot. "I wouldn't mind another magical journey. Being wished from Al-Kal'as to Tyre was the most exciting thing that ever happened to me. Next to meeting you, of course."

Hassan laughed and motioned for Sparrow to come sit by him. "A new little sister—I always wanted one," he said. "And now that Aminah and I have just such a sister, I think we have no more need of magic."

"Probably not," said Aminah. "Enchantments have kept me from living my own life far too long."

"Still, I'm glad you decided to use magic to repair my burned flesh—and Hassan's crippled leg," said Idris.

Jinni snickered, and both Hassan and Idris turned red. After a wish for Ella and another to rescue Sparrow, Aminah had had but one wish left to heal them both, and so Jinni had required them to hold hands as the spell was cast—an order they'd refused until Aminah threatened a month of swine faces instead.

Aminah turned a cool eye on Jinni, who swallowed his laughter and concentrated on devouring a roasted leg of lamb. "I thought all of you might be interested in the latest news about Ahab and Ella," she said.

"The tailor?" asked Sparrow. "And the girl with the glass slippers? Oh yes, I'd love to hear!" The others nodded.

"Well, Ahab and Kahlidah have too many orphans to count these days." Aminah threw out her arms to indicate some fathomless number. "Ahab is back to sewing like the wind and much happier for it."

"And Ella?" asked Hassan. "I always liked that girl."

"Should I be jealous?"

"If it will hurry you along with our wedding plans, then consider Ella a rival," he answered with a smile.

"I trust you too much to be jealous," she said, with a smile of her own. "Now, as for Ella, her last gift has foiled three more attempts on her life. I think her enemies are giving up. And as hoped, she's a great influence on Prince Louis, especially since they were wed. She's convinced him to create paying jobs for the poor—and schools!"

"It's a fine thing you have done with the lamp," said Aladdin. "Had I done a fraction as well, I would have saved myself much grief. I'm not sure you should stop."

"And what about me?" demanded Jinni. He pulled himself away from the haunch of meat and stood shaking a greasy finger at Aminah. "Do I not have a say in this matter? Besides, there is yet another bit of magic in which you *must* indulge. For the sake of us all—except Idris, that is. He deserves no help."

Aminah sighed. "Are you ever going to forgive him, Jinni? He meant you no harm."

Jinni shrugged. "You know what enchantment I mean," he said, ignoring her question. "And now is the time."

"He's talking about protecting us from Badr," said Aminah. "I will admit to having used the orb to keep track of her. She's ruling Al-Kal'as with an iron fist now, though she's not getting on well with Sixer. The Princess has used only one wish, but she's convinced she can force more than three out of him."

"Then Badr will think of a way to torture the creature," said Aladdin.

"Poor Sixer," said Aminah.

"Poor Sixer?" Jinni stared in disbelief. "Poor Sixer? Have you forgotten what that desiccated, malodorous, deceitful, depraved—"

"Yes, yes, you're right," said Aminah. "But unlike the Princess, Sixer has an excuse—he's a demon. And a four-digit demon at that."

"Hmmph!" Jinni grumbled.

"I shudder to think of the suffering Badr is causing in Al-Kal'as," said Aladdin. "I must find a way to stop her, though it would seem impossible."

"To see my home crushed under Badr's heel . . . I can hardly bear it, either," Aminah said. "But I agree, stopping her would take—"

"A jinni," said Jinni.

Idris laughed at Aminah's shocked expression. "You never were able to envision Jinni as a weapon," he said. "To your credit, I suppose, but you ought to consider it."

Aminah shook her head, remembering with horror what Sixer had done to the pirate ship. "No, I couldn't use him that way." She paused, glancing at Aladdin. "I simply couldn't."

"Are you sure?" asked Aladdin. The idea had kindled a fire in his eyes. "Those are our people in Al-Kal'as, Aminah. Don't say no just yet. Will you at least consider it?"

She turned to Hassan.

"You shouldn't do what feels wrong," he said. "But it can't hurt to do some thinking."

Aminah nodded. "No promises, but I will think about it."

Aladdin smiled grimly. "That's all I ask."

"And if you decide the answer is yes," said Sparrow, "perhaps Jinni could teach my uncle a lesson, too."

"Sparrow!" cried Aminah.

"I was only teasing," she said. "At least, mostly."

Jinni grunted impatiently. "Hello, everyone! There are more

pressing problems than Al-Kal'as." Forgetting he appeared as Uncle Omar, Jinni blasted purple steam from his nostrils with an earsplitting screech.

"That was magnificent!" said Sparrow. "Do it again!"

"No!" cried everyone else.

"I shall hold back my nose, but only if Aminah explains my plan to protect our dwelling from the Princess."

"Your wish is my command," said Aminah, and the demon rolled his eyes at her mocking tone. "Jinni says I can move the house to the next hillock—and make it both unseen and untouchable. We'll be the only ones to know where it is and how to get inside. That would take care of things should Badr decide to send someone after us."

"Yes," Jinni said, clapping his hands with glee. "The Princess and her men would walk right through the place without knowing it. I would like to see that miserable four-digit mongrel manage this sort of magic!"

"Oh, I don't know," said Idris. "What he did to you was very impressive."

Uncle Omar's face darkened with a deep purple stain. "That is enough from you, jailer of jinn! Burier of demons! Destroyer of—"

"Omar!" Barra stood, stamping her foot. "Let go of this grudge. Idris is merely jesting with you."

Jinni's face blanched, and he seemed to go limp. "Have your fun," he muttered.

"Go on, Idris, tell us more," said Barra.

"Even in his battered state, one could see Jinni made a fine, fine-looking pig." Idris waved his sherbet glass for emphasis.

"Such a noble snout! Such piercing, angry little eyes! Sixer's conjuring was impeccable."

When everyone laughed, Jinni gave in and laughed, too. His head suddenly disappeared with a pop, replaced by a leering swine that nuzzled Barra's cheek with its wet snout. Barra screamed, slapping the snuffling nose and coming away with pig mucus on her hand, which she ceremoniously wiped onto Uncle Omar's sleeve.

"Jinni," said Aminah, "I'm surprised and pleased you're able to laugh at this."

"Ah, I laugh now," he answered, his eyebrows furrowing, "but that vile, loathsome, pusillanimous bottle imp had better be watching his backside."

"Sixer *was* truly disgusting," Idris agreed. "Hassan, have I told you about his venting? No? Well, now . . ."

AS THE WISHING MOON crested the horizon a few nights later, Aminah used two of her three wishes. With the first, she moved the house. With the second, she created the cloaking spell.

The relocated house required some getting used to for everyone. To further ensure their safety, the cloaking spell allowed only the seven members of the Alliance of the Lamp to enter. For a guest to pass the portals, touching one of the seven was required.

However, once inside, everything seemed perfectly normal. Still, getting inside was a trick, as it was impossible to feel the walls or the gates—much less see them. In the end, Idris,

Hassan, and Aladdin marked the ways in and out using a few carefully placed stones, but whenever they all left the estate, the gates remained open. Otherwise, there was no possible way to reenter. Walking between the stone markers and into a closed gate meant walking across an empty hilltop.

Traveling into Tyre also required some adjustments. Barra's talent with needle and thread eventually supplied them with an amazing selection of disguises, which allowed them to enter the city unrecognized.

By the time the next full moon was on the horizon, life had settled into welcome routines. Aminah left the lamp untouched in her hidden closet until yet another wishing moon rose in the sky—and then another. And another.

Instead, she gave herself over to a life with Hassan. They spent many starlit evenings riding the beaches on horseback or visiting Tyre in disguise—talking nonstop about their future together. And she would have been blissfully happy but for Aladdin's unanswered plea. Like a burrowing insect, a sense of unrest about Al-Kal'as and Badr wormed its way into her heart, and as the fifth wishing moon appeared, Aminah knew what she must do.

She called together the Alliance of the Lamp, and as always, they met on the terrace after sunset. Idris was a day away from leaving for Makkah, as was Aladdin—the first to finish what he'd so long ago begun and the second to retrieve the gold he'd wisely set aside in the holy city. Aminah was relieved she'd come to a decision before the two were gone.

It was late when she asked them to meet her, but everyone came, some rubbing sleep from their eyes. Only Idris and

Aladdin seemed wide-awake—and, of course, Jinni. Ecstatic to be traveling together, Idris and Aladdin mounted the stairs, chattering enthusiastically about their journey. But as soon as they saw Aminah, they grew somber.

Sparrow couldn't keep her eyes open, and so she leaned against Barra. "Promise to wake me when something important happens," she whispered, and Barra nodded.

"Is there trouble?" asked Hassan.

"No," Aminah said. "Why would you think that?"

"Why else would you pull us from our beds?"

She looked at him in surprise. "I didn't mean to alarm anyone," she said. "I wasn't thinking, I guess."

"Hassan worries too much," said Barra. "Not that I blame him, mind you. So, little one, why are we here?"

Aminah pulled in a deep breath before beginning. "Idris and Aladdin are leaving in a day—and tomorrow night is reserved for a farewell feast. I should have done this sooner, but I kept putting it off—until my time ran out. I suppose I thought I might change my mind."

Hassan tensed. "If you're leaving again, I'm going with you," he said.

Aminah smiled. "You're imagining things, my dear. I'm not going anywhere, but I have made an important decision. Well, actually two. One of them needs your approval, Hassan."

"What has all this to do with me?" asked Jinni, surly at being pulled from the kitchen and a tray of sweetmeats. He hadn't bothered putting on a human appearance.

"A great deal," Aminah answered. "Now, for my first decision. Aladdin, I have agonized over the Princess and Al-Kal'as.

But Sixer gave me a taste of magic wielded as a weapon, and I still wake in the night hearing men's screams. I'm sorry, but I cannot use the lamp in that way."

Aladdin's face fell. He rose, moving to the edge of the terrace, and stood staring silently at the sea.

"But *you* can," she said.

He turned to face her. "You don't mean . . ."

"Yes, the lamp is yours. I should have returned it to you long ago."

"But what about Ahab? And Ella?" cried Sparrow, suddenly wide-awake. "You can't abandon them!"

"They survived—and did quite well—when the lamp was within the coffer," she answered softly. "They can do it again. This time I'll prepare them for the loss of their magic. It will make things easier."

For a few moments, no one spoke as they tried to make sense of what had just happened. Finally, Hassan broke the silence, speaking gently. "Are you sure you can live without the lamp, Aminah? I thought I'd be pleased to be rid of magic, but now I find the thought worrisome. I don't want you to be unhappy—or worse. And Sparrow has a point—maybe you shouldn't abandon Ella and Ahab when they have so much more that needs doing. And what of my bakery? And what of the others you have yet to help?"

Aminah aimed a piercing look at Jinni. "There *is* another solution. As I have recently come to know, my demon friend can choose to leave your magical skills in place. So, at Jinni's whim, Ella, Ahab, and you, Hassan, need not be abandoned."

Hassan rounded on Jinni. "You liar! All this time you let us believe a change in masters would end our gifts. Why am I not sur—"

"Outrageous!" Jinni bellowed, turning deep purple and ballooning to four times his size. He ignored Idris and loomed over Aminah. "After all we have been through together, you discard me like an empty flask! You ungrateful waif!" She cringed and covered her ears. Then, in an instant, his color lightened, and he began to deflate. "Oh, but now I see an advantage to your offer, Mistress. Perhaps Sixer shall have his comeuppance at my hand! And the Princess brought suffering down on me, as well. I shall happily make her pay."

"And make my uncle pay, too," said Sparrow, clapping her hands.

Aminah looked at them in dismay. "Don't you understand? I want to save Al-Kal'as, not seek revenge." Then she turned to Aladdin. "I'm certain you will use Jinni's power wisely in overcoming Badr—and also when you are sultan again."

Aladdin bowed. "I will be as wise as possible, and I will not disappoint. . . ." He froze, his eyes moving among the Alliance. Every face but Jinni's was rigid. "No . . . no, this won't do," he said at last. "For a thousand years and more the lamp has been a tool for selfishness and destruction— until it fell into your hands, Aminah. I won't be the one to change that. The lamp belongs with you. I will find another way."

"Are you certain?" she asked, unable to conceal the relief that swept through her.

Aladdin nodded, and it was clear to Aminah that his sacrifice was as great as hers would have been. However, she expected signs of joy from Jinni. Instead his face was conflicted. *He's disappointed at missing his chance for vengeance,* she thought sadly.

"Aladdin is right," said Barra, turning to the demon. "You have been redeemed by Aminah's kind use of the lamp, Omar. Do you really want to become your spiteful old self again? No, I don't think so."

At Barra's reproof, Jinni shrank the rest of the way to human size.

"I didn't mean to offend you," Aminah told him. "We do make a good team, after all."

Jinni crossed his arms over his chest and looked away.

"You are the best uncle a girl could ask for," she wheedled.

"A lot better than mine, that's for sure!" said Sparrow.

For the first time that evening Jinni smiled.

Turning back to Aladdin, Aminah said, "I'll help any other way I can."

"Except to leave me again!" Hassan encircled her with a protective arm.

Aminah laughed. "As I already said, I'm not going anywhere. Now, for my second decision—though there's more to it, now that I'll be keeping the lamp." She moved closer to Hassan and took both his hands in hers. "I'm going to transport Idris and Aladdin to Makkah with a wish."

"A much finer mode of travel, indeed," said Idris, rubbing his behind. "I can do without the saddle sores."

"I'll give you time to complete the pilgrimage, Idris, and then bring you both home. Can you keep busy in Makkah until he's ready, Aladdin?"

"Yes, but I should go on to Al-Kal'as. Unless . . ." He paused. "Are you saying that it's time for a wedding?"

"We should have everything ready for the ceremony when you return," she said. "If Hassan approves, that is."

"He approves!" everyone shouted.

Epilogue

I asked for you, my listeners, to be my judge when the tale was done. Now, will you or will you not condemn me, Idris, for my foolishness? Ah, I see by your smiles that you do not, and I am grateful.

Of course, much more of this story still lies in the future. I, along with A, am anxious to discover what will happen to the Princess. And I am anxious to return home for A's wedding—though I will also feel a little sad that I am not the groom.

The day before I departed for Makkah, A and I stood watching the waves roll in, and she spoke to me of magic. "Having once believed my days of power were over, I suppose I see things differently now," she told me. "It's not magic I don't trust, it's me."

"You are too hard on yourself," I said.

She laughed, though without humor. "You know better. You saw me at my worst—as lost and pitiful without enchantments as an opium eater without his drug."

"But now you know the danger, and you have become both strong and wise enough to ply the lamp safely."

"Someday, perhaps, I'll try again," she said. "I do want to make a difference in the lives of others, but right now I frighten myself."

It was then that a voice startled us. As if from nowhere, Sparrow appeared to say, "But you needn't worry! The true magic will keep you safe."

"And what is the true magic?" I asked her.

Sparrow smiled. "I am! And you, too, Idris. All of us."

A stared at the girl, almost as though she were seeing her for the first time.

"Our new little sister is right," I said. "Faith in your friends. Love, both given and received. That's the true magic."

"Yes," said A. "What's odd is that I thought I'd learned this lesson once before. But Sparrow, you've made it clearer than ever it was!"

During the night of our farewell feast, A confessed to all of us that she would have sorely missed her magic. "Your trust and support gave me the strength to consult the scrying glass again. Last night, I searched for yet another pure-hearted soul to help."

And were any of us alarmed? Concerned it might be too soon for her to fall back into her old ways? No, my friends, you must believe me when I tell you that every one of us—even her betrothed—was pleased to hear this news.

"The orb found an unusual boy for me—in a faraway time and place," she continued. "His name is Arthur, and oh, he ought to be king."

And thus ends my tale.